April 1990

APPLAUSE FOR
A LITTLE DEATH MUSIC

"Tantalizing music to the eyes of mystery readers . . . hits all the high notes and the plot races along *presto* with baffling counterpoint and a crescendo of a finale."

—Lilian Jackson Braun, author of
The Cat Who series

"This breezily written mystery gives the reader a box seat at a Florida music festival where the finale is murder. Music lovers should appreciate the author's slyly amusing impressions by egocentric concert artists and their wealthy and witless patrons."

—*St. Petersburg Times*

"A delightful, lighthearted first novel filled with lore and anecdotes from the world of music . . . blissfully succeeding on the strengths of the author's sense of humor and manic positive energy."

—*American Statesman*, Austin, TX

"A first novel and a bright, witty one. A shiny fast-moving murder mystery."

—*The Macon Beacon*

"One doesn't have to be a classical music aficionado to enjoy this novel . . ."

—*Rocky Mountain News*

"A thoroughly engaging novel of suspense."

—*Times-News*, Erie, PA

Joan Higgins

A Little Death Music

CHARTER BOOKS, NEW YORK

There is no Fun City, Florida. The locale and the events are figments of the imagination. The characters, too, are fictitious. Now they are. True, Wolfgang Amadeus Mozart might be startled to discover his rival, his doctor, his pupils, his librettist, his wife, and his brother-in-law all buried alive within. Serves them right, too.

This Charter Book contains the complete text of the original edition. It has been completely reset in a typeface designed for easy reading, and was printed from new film.

A LITTLE DEATH MUSIC

A Charter Book / published by arrangement with Dodd, Mead & Company

PRINTING HISTORY
Dodd, Mead edition published 1987
Charter edition/September 1988

ISBN: 1-55773-093-8

Charter Books are published by The Berkley Publishing Group, 200 Madison Avenue, New York, New York 10016. The name "Charter" and the "C" logo are trademarks belonging to Charter Communications, Inc.

PRINTED IN THE UNITED STATES OF AMERICA

10 9 8 7 6 5 4 3 2 1

To Mary Isabel McGarry
—in love and memory

Success is counted sweetest
By those who ne'er succeed.
To comprehend a nectar
Requires sorest need.

Not one of all the purple host
Who took the flag today
Can tell the definition
So clear of victory

As he, defeated—dying—
On whose forbidden ear
The distant strains of triumph
Burst agonized and clear!

—EMILY DICKINSON

1

TRAGEDY is always foreshadowed. Even in art. Nothing on earth happens without warning.

Looking back on it now, I realize everything was against that sudden trip to Florida. Odd harbingers cropped up at every turn, little twinges of anxiety that should have signaled alarm.

There was the matter of the plane, for one thing. I had far too much trouble catching that plane, a sure indication that I shouldn't be on it, and then there was that curious incident at the airport.

Never mind though. I did just manage to make the flight—the very last passenger aboard—on that cold, blustery November day in New York City. As the plane ascended heavenward, I heard the buzz of apprehension that swept through the cabin when the other passengers realized who was among them now. Undaunted, I strode down the aisle as confidently as I would any concert platform in the world.

"John Field!" shouted a voice from the rear of the plane. "Sit anywhere but here!"

Naturally, I recognized the corpulent form of the eminent critic Sherrill Thorne, hiding—as it were—at my approach. Naturally, I directed my steps to the empty seat next to his.

"Seriously, John," said Thorne when I reached my destination, "do you know something about this flight that we don't?"

I began to stuff my bag in the compartment overhead.

John Field
(concert piano)

"Funny you should ask," I said. My reply, unhappily, was delayed by the sharp descent of my bag on his bald head. Consternation all round, but only a slight dent to the critic's shining pate. Truth to tell, I'd long yearned to bash Sherrill Thorne in the head—a sentiment shared by all artists of my acquaintance—but fate had not been kind. Up until now.

"Pity," I said, by way of apology. "Lucky for you that bag contains only shirts and socks. I checked everything else, even my piano-tuning equipment, on through."

This statement was uttered somewhat regretfully, but Thorne chose to interpret the tone as jocular. He pushed the corners of his lips upward—much as a wolf would bare its fangs—and he said tightly, "How about your black cloud? Did you pack that along, too?"

Clearly, Thorne was somewhat pettish after that nasty blow on the head. Next thing you know, he would deliver his pronunciamento, "Wherever John Field is, there also is murder."

So I let the cloud remark pass—he, of all people, should know my bag was heavier than air—and I let worry consume me about the fate of my baggage.

Quite true, I really *had* checked those heavy tools on through and with the utmost reluctance at the time. Violinists, clarinetists, even harpists, my God, carry their instruments around with them from place to place. But until a concert pianist reaches the rarefied stratosphere of an Artur Rubinstein, he simply can't carry around a Steinway.

Even the best of us—and I include myself in that category—are presented deathtraps disguised as pianos on the concert stage. My solemn word, I have encountered bêtes noires that have missing keys, broken pedals, and occasionally even an absence of the entire bass register.

So I've learned. If the piano isn't tuned, and it seldom is, I tune it myself. If the tone still isn't there, I simply *will* it into being. And let me tell you, I hug that piano-tuning kit to my breast as lovingly as Heifetz does his Stradivarius. Or, in this instance, as Sherrill Thorne his Valium. He was stuffing tranquilizers into his mouth at the speed of sound, a gesture I could not but take personally.

He was, by the way, perfectly serious in his question about the flight. There have been—how shall I put it?—incidents, to the distress of my management and avid listeners everywhere.

Such are the perils of air travel today. If you've time to spare, go by air. As they say.

With just the slightest memory nudge, Thorne might easily have brought up that outrageous detainment in East Germany when I failed utterly to even *see* the Berlin Wall, never mind march across it undetected. (Management always fails to provide adequate street maps for any city.)

Inevitably, this would loose dark statements about "murder most foul" and my being "Johnny-on-the-spot." In my opinion, the really foul part about it is that I am always left, as it were, holding the bag.

At the moment, America's dean of music critics was holding his head. He rubbed the small though rapidly enlarging bump on his cranium and resumed our conversation.

"You were saying, John?"

"Oh, yes, I started to say that it was funny you should ask about this flight."

"Why is that funny?" Thorne looked uneasy.

"Because I'm not supposed to be on it."

"What plane were you supposed to be on?"

I detected the nervous edge in Sherrill's voice, but I was busy looking out the window and too preoccupied to reassure him. One likes to check on all the motors, if only to ascertain that they are there, before relaxing into one's seat.

"What? . . . Oh, yes," I said. "I was supposed to be on that Israel Airways plane, the one that left last night for Jerusalem."

"And landed this morning in Chad? Is that the one you mean?"

"Now that you mention it—yes, I believe that there was some such detour. Sherrill, why are you crouching down in your seat like that?"

Thorne ran a furtive hand over his head and asked, "Not to press the point, John, but did you bother to cancel your reservations?"

"Management tends to those details, I assume." Mentally, I reflected on their street maps. "Along with telling me, twenty minutes before flight time, that the performance has been canceled and that the Israel Philharmonia is on strike."

"They found out you were coming, that's what happened! They didn't want to lose their entire string section to bubonic plague. Thank God—if there is a God—nobody knows you're here! Are you *sure* about that?''

"Relax, Sherrill. You have absolutely nothing to worry about." I lowered my voice to a whisper to balance the hysteria in his.

"Nobody—not even my management—knows that I'm here."

"Why not?" He still looked ashen.

John "Because I'm substituting for Eric Hanson, a last-minute favor. He was bitten in the leg by a dog last night. Nothing serious—just a nick. But you know what a fuss the doctors make until they find the dog."

No need to mention the ironic coincidence that the dog bit Eric at the same hour that my scheduled flight ascended—8:05 P.M. to the minute.

My phone was ringing off the hook when I returned last night to my West Side apartment. There was Eric on the other end, pleading, cajoling, and describing in graphic detail his bleeding stump of a leg. Or so he said—"bleeding stump." Astute questioning on my part confirmed the suspicion that the bite barely pierced the skin, and we all know what a hypochondriac Eric is.

"Please, John, you've got to do this one favor for me. You've helped me out before, I know, and I'm truly sorry about what happened last time."

What happened last time was this. Last year, Eric came down suddenly with the flu, and I took one of his engagements on very short notice. By then, there was no time to change his name to mine on the printed program.

Music criticism being what it is today, the local critic didn't know my face from Eric's (I have a blond beard, he does not), nor did she arrive in time to hear the announced substitution. So the unhappy result of my last favor for Eric was that *he* got the glowing review, the string of engagements based on that review, and the deep-seated conviction that it had been he, all along, who played so beautifully that night. Good deeds, as Hegel put it so well, do not go unpunished.

These recollections came to mind as Eric babbled on. I listened to him in stony silence.

"John, you *know* that Yera Concerto! You know it better than I do! You premiered it, for Chrissake!"

I was mute.

"It's too late for me to call anybody in Fun City! Too late to cancel and too late to let them down! It's the biggest shindig they've ever had in Florida!"

Eric is often prone to exaggeration. How could he forget about the opening of Disney World?

"This is a *special* performance," he continued, "for special givers! Wonderful exposure! Everybody from the mayor on down will be there!"

"How far down can you go from the mayor?" I knew all about Fun City—riots, murders, corruption, drug dealing, unspeakable, horrendous crimes.

But that reply—any reply at all—indicated a chink in my armor. He sensed I was weakening. He knows I love the work.

Finally, the coup de grâce: "John, you know perfectly well there are only two pianists in the world who can play that wristbreaker!"

"Sorry, you're wrong. Many could. They need only apply themselves."

"Yes, but we're the only ones who've mastered it! It took me a solid year to get it in my fingers! How long did it take you?"

I thought a minute and replied, "It took me five weeks."

"You're kidding!"

"No—five weeks. The Yera Concerto is the most difficult work I've ever encountered as a professional musician, and it took me the longest time to conquer."

"Jeez." This last in a whisper. His voice was running out of exclamation points.

"I'll be honest with you, John." He took a long breath, and I sensed an admission coming that would cost him dearly.

"You play it better than I do."

Well. I could hardly argue that point. But I know, too, that musicians must never admit weakness, especially to themselves.

"Nonsense, Eric. You play it every bit as well as I do. Our conceptions are different, that's all. You play it like the contemporary work that it is, and I—"

"You play it—like Chopin. That's how you play it. That's the way new music should be played—as if it were the work of an old master. That much care should be lavished on it."

I cut him off gruffly. He was saying things he would regret tomorrow, things damaging to the necessarily massive ego of a pianist.

"Eric, go back to bed. Of course I'll fill in for you. Just take care of yourself. I hope they find the dog."*

* They did. The next day. A Pekingese of impeccable pedigree, with all her shots.

2

So it was that I came to be on this plane, chartered and paid for by the wealthy patrons of the Yera Festival. But although my presence here could be easily accounted for, Sherrill Thorne's could not. Wasn't it he who had stated categorically, "There is no civilization south of Philadelphia?" Meant it, too. Yet here he was—venturing far south of the Mason-Dixon line, far beyond the pale of cultural life as we know it today.

I turned to ask him to explain this anomaly, but his eyes were tightly closed. Lulled by the ceaseless hum of the plane's motors, Thorne had nodded off to dreamland. I didn't blame him. The man's almost eighty now and all but retired, though an occasional piece still appears in the *New York Globe* under the title "Critic Emeritus."

These little naps, gossip had it, had hastened his retirement. Rumors reached me that Thorne was constantly pitching forth from his seat at concerts—sound asleep—and was then writing scathing reviews or what he could not possibly have heard. He was always awake and biting at *my* concerts, so I considered the rumors unfounded.

In my opinion, both his ear and his eye were as sharp as ever. Thorne noticed things. A highly observant man. I had meant to ask him if, from his seat next to the window, he had witnessed that odd confrontation on the runway.

7

I had come so close to missing the flight that by the time I reached the gate, our craft was loaded and warming up on the tarmac.

As I ran toward the plane, a burly flight mechanic emerged from beneath the wings and rushed away from it. We almost collided, but I veered to the right just in time.

"Is that the plane to Fun City?" I shouted the question to him above the din of the motors.

He turned a glance of such hatred and malevolence down on me that I realized he hadn't heard the question at all.

"Fun City?" I repeated. Suddenly he smiled, nodded, and pointed a tattooed forearm toward the plane. He even joined me in flagging the pilot, who finally noticed me and ordered the door opened. Minutes later, we were airborne. No reason, but I found the entire incident disquieting.

Now that we were above the fog and well on our way, I looked around the cabin and surveyed the passengers. Quite a stellar cast was here. If anything happened to this plane, I reflected bleakly, a black hole would open up in the international music world. There was James Goldman, the great violinist; Nicholas Rouse, the eminent violist; Frederick Rheinwein, the cellist of renown. I waved at them and the four other musicians—seven in all, of the finest instrumentalists in Europe and America. I knew them all, had even recorded the Yera Concerto with them some years back. (The Yera Concerto, by the way, is not a concerto at all but is simply called that for want of a more descriptive term. It is a work for eight performers—seven instrumentalists and one singer—and all eight must be virtuosos of the highest order.)

Unfortunately, I didn't know the conductor or the contralto for this performance, and I failed, through the process of elimination, to spot them here. Probably they were already in Fun City, but I yearned to know who they were. Those two would be in fast company tonight.

Directly across the aisle sat a dark-haired girl of twenty or so, dressed in gabardine ski pants and armed with a hand calculator. I wondered—with that half-conscious attention one gives passing thoughts—how she had broken her foot. Was she returning home after the mishap, or was she en route to Vail, via Florida, in order to break the other foot? The cast, you can see, offered many plausible explanations, but I was totally flummoxed by the hand calculator. Was she calculating the cost of her medical expenses to date?

Apparently I was staring, for the young beauty reacted to my undivided attention with a glance that qualified easily as a glare. I quickly averted my eyes. And a good thing, too. I was fairly blinded by her ice-blue gaze, which lit up the cabin.

So. This chartered flight wasn't quite as chartered as I had been led to believe. Not if we were taking on skiers for ballast. Or maybe we had one stowaway in this plane-load of musicians.

It was then I noticed an anemic-looking youngster of the Botticelli stamp. I counted the passengers again. One stowaway I could accept, but . . . let's see, seven performers of the eight required, one critic not at all required, one contralto unaccounted for, and one conductor. . . . My heart sank to the pit of my stomach and straight down to the tip of my right toe.

I jabbed Sherrill Thorne sharply in the ribs. He had slept long enough.

"Who *is* that twit?" I asked, shaking him a little.

"What twit? Which twit?"

"The one between Connacht and Holzman!"

"Oh"—light dawned—"between the flutist and the clarinetist. Why didn't you say so?"

He paused and peered closely.

"That's Luciano Lacramose, your conductor."

"Never heard of him."

"Known throughout the music world—or the seamier sides of it—as 'Comatose Lacramose.' "

"God in Heaven above!" I crossed myself.

"Also known as 'Lazy Lazarus.' When I heard him last— and I devoutly hoped that was the last time I'd hear him—I mistakenly called him 'Lazarus' in my review, a Freudian slip on my part, but the tag stuck on in the musical underworld. To tell you the truth, I was not at all sure, based on that single performance, that he hadn't really risen from the dead."

In a state of shock, I stood up and walked to the front of the cabin to seek out James Goldman, a violinist noted as much for his steely nerve as for his rich tone. On the way, I took a closer look at Lacramose. One guarded view of the angelic face, the vacant eyes, the black locks curling down the slim neck, and my apprehension deepened.

"Goldy," I said, "I need some reassurance."

"You've seen our conductor?"

"I have. Know anything at all about him?"

"Not much. I've never played under his baton. No one here has. He's supposed to have excellent credentials. On paper."

We both knew how worthless that recommendation was.

Goldy went on: "You thought Dmitri Polopolis was conducting. So did I, when I accepted this engagement. Dmitri dropped dead yesterday in Athens. That news missed the late editions. A friend phoned me about it just before I caught this plane."

Fate was up to her old tricks again, it seemed to me, and Goldy must have seen the dismay etched on my face. "One consolation for all of us. Dmitri knew Yera's works backward and forward. This fellow—Lacramose, is it?—was *very* close to him. Apprenticed conducting with him in Paris."

"Are you sure conducting was what he apprenticed?"

We exchanged knowing glances. No need to dwell on all the "conductors" that Dmitri Polopolis had loosed upon the world. They were all of the same stamp—bloodless Adonises who had one engagement, one disaster, before returning to the nameless oblivion from whence they came.

My luck was holding true.

"Why worry?" asked Goldman. "We can do without him if we have to."

"*We* could, but could the contralto? I don't even know who's singing. Do you?"

"I think it's Kirsten Waglock. My God, no! She's singing at the Met tonight!" Goldman's composure had quickly deserted him and was now marching right along with my despair.

"Go back and ask Thorne. He knows everything!"

I hurried back, as suggested. But when I reached my seat, Thorne was fast asleep. So was the girl with the X-ray eyes. I took a long look at that young face—not a line in it—and I considered how unlikely a stowaway was on this plane filled with distinguished musicians.

Could this be our contralto?

3

THERE was nothing for it but to read the *Fun City Sun*, which the stewardess had thoughtfully placed in my seat during my restless foray through the cabin. So I sat down.

At my side, Thorne was sleeping off the effects of several double Scotches and the tranquilizers he'd been consuming like candy since the moment I joined him. Liquor + Valium + Me = Trouble. Right here, or close to, Fun City. Still, I thought, if Thorne could live as long as he already had, he surely knew the strengths and weaknesses of his own body.

At any rate, a Thorne *at* my side was a pleasant change from a Thorne *in* my side, and not for the first time I pondered how an otherwise reasonable man could make his living as a critic.

Criticism is, all things considered, the profession of a parasite. Has to be. You live by feeding off the talent of others. The temptations to do so, of course, must be enormous. To name but one: security. You'll never be jobless as long as someone else has talent. To name another: glory. That's the very best thing of all. Everybody knows about you in the small, elitist circle of music; nobody at all knows about you in the outside world. And that, to hear critics tell it, is just the way they want it. Homage is welcome, but only from those with master's degrees.

In the major cultural cities, critics can even develop little

cults and coteries of devotees who think (if they think at all)
just like them. Well, *chacun à son goût*. As they say. Off-
hand, I can't think of any drawback at all to pursuing a career
as a critic, barring all those guitar recitals one must inevitably
hear.

But make no mistake about it, critics are powerful. They
may know little, they may earn less, yet within their small
orbits, they act as Lord High Executioners. And until such
time as a performer gets out of their reach and into the sun
of success, he runs the risk that at any time, and for no
apparent reason, a critic who knows little and understands
nothing will smash his career as recklessly and as blithely as
boys kill flies on hot summer days.

One comforting thing I noted as I read the *Fun City Sun*:
whatever else that newspaper had, it certainly had no music
critic. What it had was a staff of sports writers covering the
rest of the news as best it could. Although this worked well
for international coverage (HIJACKERS SCORE AGAIN) and for
the food section (DIVE INTO APRICOTS), it failed abysmally in
describing the Yera Festival. Clearly, the staff felt out of its
depth in describing a cultural event of this magnitude and so
consequently dumped the entire job on its society editor.

Her article and byline appeared—probably for the first and
last time in her life—on page one:

ON THE TOWN
By TABBIE TURNER

Our town is bracing for its first Yera Music Festival
ever as prominent arts patrons welcome internationally
acclaimed musicians to Fun City for the dedication of
the Antonio Saul Yera Arts Center.

Tonight the Yera Concerto, by Fun City's own cele-
brated Tony Yera, will be performed at Harmonia's Hall
of Mirrors by the same musicians who introduced it to
the world ten years ago, and who have since embarked
on brilliant solo careers of their own. You can imagine
what a bundle their fees are costing the Arts Committee!

Following intermission, our local musicians will
perform Haydn's *Farewell Symphony* (on which Tony

based his concerto*) in a re-creation of its original eighteenth-century setting. Candlelight will illuminate the Hall of Mirrors in Fun City's new arts center, and the musicians will wear livery, the uniform of service donned by musicians and other servants in Haydn's day.

After the performance, Tony will hand over the keys of Harmonia, his very own personal mansion, to Fun City residents for their use as the Antonio Saul Yera Arts Center. The city, for its part, will deed Tony a separate wing and a life estate in Harmonia, and upon his death (which we all hope won't be for years and years yet), the entire estate will revert to Fun City.

Conversion of Harmonia to an arts center complex has been going on for months now. Town officials have already transferred the entire municipal library to Harmonia, and the city has shared some of the costs in restoring this glorious old mansion on Key Cohen.

But the real vote of thanks, both for the soon-to-be-yearly Yera Festival and for the enlargement of the Hall of Mirrors into a performance center, goes to all those Fun Cityites who have contributed so much of their time and money to this new endeavor.

In appreciation, donors of $100,000 or more will be honored tonight at the invitation-only gala performance at Key Cohen. Chairman Connie Weber wants to extend a special thanks to the board members, each of whom gave at least $300,000 to the new center. Besides herself, these include her "special pal" Miguel Ochelly from Colombia; World War II hero General Vance Sweeten and his wife Frieda; Fun City's leading (and only) impresario, Rachael Radler, and her spouse, banker Richard Radler; Robert O'Reilly, that handsome and so-eligible lawyer; Salvaniguan Consul Armando Argento and his delicious Alicia; the famed painter Joseph Lange; and Police Commissioner Lorenzo DaPonto and his better half, Lisa.

Pressed on how the rest of us can aspire to become a board member of the new Yera Center, Connie re-

---

* Tabbie's a tad wrong. Yera has used Bach, Mozart, even Schumann as a model. Haydn, never.

plied, "Just give $300,000 or more, honey, and you're an automatic member."

What a card is our real estate tycoonness! And how much we owe Connie and her crew!

The most disturbing part of the entire account—aside from the arch writing—was the revelation of where, exactly, we would perform. A Hall of Mirrors. Have you got any idea what happens to acoustics in a glass-lined hall?

I was about to tax Sherrill Thorne, asleep or not, with this new abomination when the stewardess spared me the trouble by bringing our dinners. Thorne stirred, and I heard his resonant bass voice, now hushed and respectful, in my ear.

"You actually know him, don't you?" he asked.

"Who?"

"Antonio Saul Yera. You've met him, talked to him, performed with him."

"I can't deny that. He conducted the world premiere of the Yera Concerto some years back, and I was the piano soloist."

Thorne then supplied the exact date, the time of the performance, the weather in Paris on the day in question. All this is very important to critics. I don't quite know why.

"It was just after you'd won the Leeds International Competition in England," he reminded me. "Quite a coup for a young pianist to play Yera's first major work in years."

"Yes," I sighed nostalgically. "Do you realize there have been ten winners at Leeds since then? All of us now competing for the same concert halls and the same audiences? I don't really see how we can deal with the population explosion on the planet until we address the question of the burgeoning outbreak of pianists."

"Ah, yes," replied Thorne. "Mercifully, there are few artists among them, so I don't see why you should worry about them. Getting back to Yera—"

Thorne's eyes shone with the zeal of a fanatic, and I remembered just in time that Thorne was considered the world's authority on Antonio Saul Yera.

"I'm writing the definitive biography, you know, of America's greatest composer," he began.

"But the man's not dead yet!"

"Hanging on by a thread, they say. A human cadaver, the last I heard. Naturally, it's a great privilege to meet the Master in the flesh. While it's still warm, one might say. I need to check out certain biographical facts, artistic developments. From the horse's mouth, so to speak. And it would help a lot—" To my great amazement, Sherrill Thorne seemed on the point of stammering. "It would help a lot," he continued, "if you would—"

"Translate?" I suggested.

"Well, it's like talking to Beethoven, you know. What does one *say?*"

"Do you mean to tell me, Sherrill, that in all your years as a critic you've never interviewed Antonio Yera?"

"Antonio *Saul* Yera," he corrected me. "His mother was Jewish. No, dear boy, I've never really had the chance. While he was conducting and composing in New York, I was performing and reviewing in London."

"Performing?" I asked, all agog. "You were a—?" I waited expectantly.

"Singer. Bass baritone."

"Operatic?"

"Ummmm, yes."

"What roles?"

"Do you want your roll, by the way? I see you haven't touched it."

"Help yourself. What roles? Covent Garden, I assume," I added maliciously.

"Oh, Covent Garden, to be sure. The chorus, if you must know. The fact is that as a young man, I had aspirations to be a singer. But what with one thing and another, I turned to writing instead."

He then outlined in tedious detail his reasons for escaping from the chorus: inadequate pay, long hours, the hideous behavior of the company's leading tenor. I barely listened, flushed as I was with the triumph of having beaten out the truth that underlined a natural law—that most critics are failed musicians.

When next I tuned in, Sherrill was still outlining the sins of the tenor. "Gambled away every cent of his own money, mind you, then had to come to the chorus for the plane fare to the next city on the tour. And the tours were another thing.

They stuck you in hotels without running water or heat and expected you to sing like angels the next night.''

All these, you understand, were the standard complaints of opera choristers the world over. Never stopped Dame Janet Baker, to name but one gifted singer who started in the Covent Garden chorus and aspired heavenward.

But on the basis of Thorne's brief, unhappy stint at about the lowest possible echelon of music, on the basis of that "professional experience" and a glib tongue, he'd been judging me and others like me for years. I listened with half an ear as Thorne slowly wended his tortuous way back from his early trials and tribulations to his later trials and tribulations.

That subject exhausted, the critic turned to the life of his idol. Finally, we were back home again with a summary of the greatest exploits, artistic and otherwise, of the great Antonio Yera during his New York period, as Sherrill termed it.

"He really brought public attention to the works of Anton Bruckner, which had been rarely performed until then. Imagine, he was a mere youth, still in his thirties, and already a great conductor."

"That was before my time," I began.

"Not really," said Thorne. "You were at least born. You must have heard the tunes of his Broadway musicals as a child."

"Now that you mention it, I did. They were among my earliest encounters with music. I still think 'When It's Springtime in Wyoming' was one of the greatest songs ever written for Broadway. All of his Broadway musicals, in fact, are classics of the genre to this day. You know, I've always wondered how Antonio Yera could turn his back on that lucrative popular success of his early years and devote himself with such passion and dedication to serious composition."

"Well, for one thing," said Thorne, "he had all the money anyone could need. You know the astronomical fees of a good conductor. In his day, Yera was the most sought-after conductor of them all. Add to that the enormous popular success of his musicals, and I imagine he's still getting royalties from them. Then he inherited fortunes from both his mother and father. Indeed, Yera must be the wealthiest composer in the history of music.

"Money didn't mean anything to him," continued Thorne,

"but real artistic achievement did. He had to have that to survive. And he got it at last by holing up—there's no other word for it—in Florida."

"What happened then?"

"Well, the complete vacuum of intellectual life there forced him to develop his own inner resources."

"You mean, forced him—like Haydn—to be original?"*

"A lot like Haydn, though I never would have thought of that comparison. But his isolation turned the trick. That and giving up women. For a time, anyway."

"How many times was he married?" I asked.

"Four, I think. Or was it five? That's one of the things I want to ask him about. To be quite honest, I lost count somewhere in the middle. One love couldn't get a divorce, and that was the most tempestuous affair of all."

"He had a pronounced weakness for singers, didn't he?"

"Sopranos, mostly. There were, of course, exceptions along the way. Mary Calnan was his first wife. Tried to lose the girth that every singer needs and lost her voice, her career, and her husband instead. I know she's supposed to have died of a heart ailment. But at thirty-nine? I'll always think she committed suicide, never mind what the papers reported."

I really didn't want to know any more about Antonio Saul Yera's love life, but it was apparent that Sherrill Thorne was warming to his subject.

"Wife Number Two was Mary Calnan's greatest rival—Regina Dulcino, the great lyric spinto. She died in a car accident within a year after their marriage, just before she was to have made her debut at the Metropolitan Opera. Naturally, both Calnan and Dulcino left their money to Yera—as if he needed it!"

"What about his third wife?" In spite of myself, I felt compelled to ask the question. "Who was she?"

* Franz Josef Haydn (1732–1809) served as court composer for the royal household of Prince Esterhazy in Eisenstadt, Austria, for thirty years. His isolation from the intellectual currents of Vienna forced him into individual and brilliant solutions of musical problems in all branches of composition.

"Oh, some little nothing. The lead in one of his Broadway musicals, I think. I wouldn't know the name."

Nor would Sherrill think that achievement of any importance.

"And she wasn't so little, either," he continued. "Towered over Yera, I'm told. Why are conductors so universally short?"

I glared at him. Frankly, I'm not so terribly tall myself.

"Something compensatory at work there," he went on, answering his own question. "No, his third wife broke with tradition, in a sense. A singer, but not an operatic singer. No match for him intellectually. Not that opera singers are heavyweights in the brain department, usually."

"Maybe Yera tired of temperament," I suggested.

"Married her twice, if memory serves."

"Was there someone else in between?" I was beginning to sound like a journalist for *People*.

"Oh, yes, an immensely talented woman. What was her name?"

"Another soprano?"

"No. Far too clever. Let me think. . . . I remember! She was a brilliant but erratic pianist, and she had a very hokey name."

I named any number of women pianists, all of whom might fall into the category that Thorne reserved for pianists who were not men—"the erratic but brilliant Emily Lash," "the brilliantly erratic Margaret Richelieu"—the list was endless, but none of them woke a chord of response in Thorne.

"Began with a G," he said. "Last name had a lot of L's."

This narrowed the field. I suggested Gloria Languidere, just to see if he was napping, and this prodded his memory.*

"Theresa von Trattner! That's who it was! Do you know the name?"

"Good God, Sherrill, of course I know the name. Every pianist knows that name.† If I believed in definitive record-

---

* Possibly because it was too hokey. Princess Languidere was the character in the *Oz* stories who put on a new head each day.
† Though Thorne was right that her moniker was somewhat fishy. The first recorded Theresa von Trattner was a pupil—and possibly a lover—of Wolfgang Amadeus Mozart. I would imagine that an imaginative

ings, I would say that Theresa von Trattner made them all. She bred a whole generation of pianists—of which I am but one—just as Fritz Kreisler bred a generation of violinists. All through their recordings.''

''Your Trattner recordings must be collector's items now. There just weren't that many.''

''There were twenty-four. Exactly. I have them all, and I treasure each one. Tell me, Sherrill, is it substantiated truth or just idle gossip that Theresa von Trattner was one of Yera's inamoratas? I've never heard that before.''

''Absolutely true, dear boy. Lived with him for a couple of years. Anybody can tell you that. She went to him as a conducting pupil, I believe, after her career as a pianist came to such an abrupt end.''

I recalled that the legendary pianist had developed a form of neurosis in her left hand that defied diagnosis and cure. She lost all use of the hand, as though it had been blown off.

''Nothing much came of her conducting studies,'' continued Thorne, ''except, of course, a notorious love affair that virtually cured Antonio Saul Yera of women forever. Or so everybody thought.''

''What happened? Yera certainly had proved he was the marrying kind. Why didn't she marry him?''

''She didn't have time,'' said Thorne reflectively. ''Yera finally got his divorce, but not Theresa. Her husband fought it violently. And I knew him—he was just that kind. Greedy, possessive, what the youngsters today call macho. But then, I've already described his character. Eventually, he behaved true to form. True to his destructive nature, I mean.''

''What did he do?''

''He waited for Antonio and Theresa to return to Harmonia, which had just been built, and he kidnapped his wife. His ex-wife, by that time.''

''And then?'' I prompted.

''Murdered her. You mean to tell me you don't know any of this? It was one of the most sensational scandals of the day. Where were you?''

agent baptized the twentieth-century Theresa von Trattner. Or at least threw in the ''von,'' since the pianist was Kansas-born.

"In the arms of innocence, since you ask. You know perfectly well I was a child at that time. Get on with the story."

"Well, to continue, Theresa's husband took her out on a boat, then sunk the boat with both of them on it. Horrible, absolutely horrible. Yera was forced to identify the body of his mistress—or what was left of it after the sharks had visited the scene—and he never got over it. He left the New York scene permanently and moved down here. That's when he settled down to being a serious composer."

"If he was so grief-stricken, why did he remarry? One assumes he divorced Wife Number Three, or she him, because of mutual dislike."

"As a matter of fact, that's one of the many things I want to ask him. I hope you'll help me phrase that question tactfully."

"From all you've told me, Sherrill, I don't think it was opera singers who attracted him."

"No?"

"On the contrary, the man casts himself in his own dramas. And they're all soap operas with the woman lead written right out of the script. I would think that any woman who feels herself even remotely drawn to Antonio Yera would drop everything and run for her life. What happened to his third wife, by the way?"

"I've no idea. If she were alive, she'd be a little long in the tooth for Broadway."

"*If* she were alive, that would indeed be true. Given Yera's record with women, her life expectancy must rank low on a life insurance chart. I will admit that I find it very hard to believe—simply because I don't want to believe it—that Theresa von Trattner was one of the trophies in that Bluebeard's Castle."

"Bluebeard's *Castle!*" Too late did I realize that I had stepped on the toes of one of Thorne's gods. "Antonio Saul Yera—a great composer, a peerless conductor, one of the masters of twentieth-century music—and you're calling him Bluebeard! Why, any woman should be honored . . ." Thorne continued on in this vein, with neck arteries bulging ominously. I had no wish to send his blood pressure up any further, so I retreated diplomatically.

"Whom had she been married to, by the way?"

"You mean Theresa von Trattner?"

"Yes," I said guilelessly, knowing full well that Sherrill Thorne, like old people the world over, had a failing memory for names and an absolute compulsion to get them right, no matter what he put others through.

"Let me think. I know it as well as I know my own . . ."

He put his head between his hands and squeezed his eyelids shut.

"Should remember, he died owing me money," he mumbled, and in no time at all Winken, Blinken, and Nod had done their work and averted Thorne's apoplexy in the process. The man really could fall asleep at the drop of a pin, pen, or pan.

That accomplished, I started to reach for my French paperback and settle down with a little Balzac when I felt two eyes boring through me like hot coals. I looked around and caught the ski-suited dark beauty across the aisle staring at me with intense concentration. For the moment, she had even banished her hand calculator.

What can I tell you? These things happen. I am not, after all, unknown. And although a public man suffers the usual penalties for fame—loss of anonymity, privacy, and so on—there are certain compensations. Occasionally.

My brief glance, catching her long stare, told me much that I had missed before. It was a face not easy to forget. It disobeyed all the rules of beauty and set up new ones in their place. High cheekbones, for example. Wide brow. The incongruity of those intelligent eyes and those sensual lips. Remarkable eyes, as I mentioned. Turn a man to stone if he looked directly in them. Long, silky black hair around alabaster features.

"I beg your pardon—"

It was as if a Munch painting had just come to life. I started visibly.

"Yes?" I smiled a regal smile, warm yet reserved.

"Aren't you . . ." she began hesitantly.

Of course I was. How could my features—distinguished, I am told—possibly be mistaken for anybody else's?

"Am I . . . ?" All God-like affability, I helped her along. Gave her the full dose of my face, now that my profile had been absorbed.

"Aren't you," she plunged ahead, "uncomfortable in these cramped seats?"

My smile faded slowly. Uncomfortable? *Uncomfortable?* Inconsolable was much more like it. For the merest moment, I was crushed and trodden. It's one thing not to be recognized in a hockey stadium. But here? On this plane? With all these musicians, none more famous than I?

A fraction of a second was needed for me to gather my resources and answer her. I considered what options were open in casting my reply. Sarcasm? Humor? Noblesse oblige? I chose the last.

"Musicians are used to uncomfortable traveling conditions. It's an occupational hazard, you know. Even Madame Schumann-Heinck—at the height of her career—used to pack a lunch and travel by third-class railway cars to out-of-the-way destinations. She considered that her responsibility. Part of the package in having a great voice in the first place.

"Of course," I continued, "traveling with a cast on your foot must be exceedingly painful, Miss . . . uh, Miss—?"

Obediently, she dug into her purse and placed a small business card in my hand, which certainly explained the calculator in hers. Imprinted on the card were the words:

HEDDA HASSE

REALTOR-ASSOCIATE

FUN IN THE SUN REALTY, INC.

FUN CITY, FLORIDA

"What a relief!" I cried, tossing noblesse oblige to wild abandon.

"Relief?" She looked quizzical.

"Forgive me," I said, trying to keep outright glee from totally suffusing my voice. "I thought for a minute you might be the contralto for tonight's performance. Ridiculous, I know. But I will admit my blood ran cold at the thought! All these international musicians, and an unknown to complete the ensemble! You'd simply have to be a musician yourself to recognize the predicament. . . ."

A waft of cold air seemed suddenly to envelop the cabin. Possibly because I had stopped talking. Possibly because she wasn't saying anything at all. Probably because her remarkable blue eyes had become cold and glacial, lowering the temperature for miles around.

"I *am* the contralto for tonight's performance," she said in a tight voice. Her voice, I will admit, was low and deep and melodious, but speaking voices don't often match singing voices.

"But . . . but . . . *why?*" Hardly the most tactful of questions.

"The composer asked me to sing it."

"Antonio Saul Yera asked *you* to sing? But you sell . . .'" I floundered helplessly.

"Real estate? That's true. I have to support myself somehow. And right now, I don't know if I'm sufficiently talented to make my living as a singer."

That was not what I wanted to hear. First the conductor. Now this. And Lacramose—never mind his technical failings—obviously had the confidence of a lion. Sometimes that confidence can even substitute for ability. The point is, though, you can't perform without it. And here our singer-cum-realtor was admitting to having all the self-assurance of a titmouse.

"Have you sung the part before?" I tried to suppress the betraying quaver in my voice.

"Not professionally, Mr. Field. It should be some consolation to you that the composer was my singing coach and that he's taken me, step by step, through every nuance of the part."

"Naturally, that is most consoling. Just to know you've practiced the interaction of the voice with all the other instruments—"

"Oh no, I haven't done that. Mr. Yera just played a piano reduction, and I just sort of sang along."

After that sally, there seemed little to say. Things, I thought, just couldn't get worse. I went right on thinking that until I heard the girl next door speak once more.

"Listen!"

I listened, but all I could hear was the plane humming and Thorne snoring.

"Isn't that a B flat?"

She couldn't mean Thorne. She must mean the plane.

"That's the F above middle C," I replied. Whatever else she had, she didn't have perfect pitch.

"*Now* it is. It's been high C all the way down. Now the tone has dropped. Why did it drop? We can't be landing yet."

I listened. She was right.

Under more auspicious circumstances, I'd have been impressed with her ear. Right now, I was noticing that, along with the hum of the motors, the entire plane was dropping.

I gazed past Thorne's vast belly to the scene from the plane's window. All I could see was endless blue sea—much closer than before—and what looked to be sharks' fins glinting in the sunlight.

Suddenly, the plane's motors coughed and sputtered. Then no sound at all from those powerful engines.

No doubt about it.

We were ditching over the Atlantic Ocean.

4

ABRUPTLY, the captain's disembodied voice filled the cabin.

"Ladies and gentlemen"—so cheerful was his voice, you'd think he was announcing the afternoon's movie—"we gotta li'l spot of trouble in the cockpit here."

More than in the cockpit. Notice the plane.

"Our oil gauges don't seem to be registerin' any oil. Now, just 'cause ya don't hear the engines and we seem to be descendin', ah don't want y'all to worry—"

Judging from the murmur that was sweeping the cabin, all of us seemed to be worried to the point of panic.

"I've shut off all the engines on purpose to conserve any oil we've still got, and I'll be startin' them up any minute now."

Soon, soon, make it soon!

"Right now, we're goin' to dump as much fuel and baggage as we need to keep this here thing aloft. Then we're goin' to take her right into Fun City. Now I want y'all to listen to the stewardesses and do like they tell ya."

The grim-faced attendants, not nearly as jovial as the captain, showed us quickly where the exits were, and the rubber rafts, and the life preservers under the seats. And we who had so blithely ignored their little spiels before now watched closely as the stewardesses demonstrated the fetal position that would miraculously protect us from eighty-seven tons of disintegrating metal.

I looked out the window and saw the fuel spilling out. But that didn't reverse the plane's downward plunge. Then I saw my own bag, the one filled with piano-tuning equipment, spilling down into the sea. That seemed to help. The plane rose perceptibly, a few hundred feet, at least.

To our combined relief, we heard the plane's motors start up again. We were gliding about five hundred feet above the Atlantic at this point, and I could now clearly discern that what I had thought were sharks' fins from a distance were in fact sharks' fins up close.

Thorne was still sleeping peacefully. Can you believe it? I shook him to try to wake him up.

"It's all right, folks." The captain's voice came on the intercom again. "The motors are workin' fine, and we're jes' gonna zoom on into Fun City. They're all waitin' for us there!"

And at last the whoop went up! We had all kept hope firmly suppressed, even when the motors started up again, but nothing could keep that cry of elation down now.

"Hooray!" cried the stewardess, and out of nowhere she produced champagne and glasses for us.

"Hooray!" shouted a sleepy Sherrill Thorne, quickly joining in the spirit of the occasion. And the spirits, too. "More!" he cried, bolting down the champagne and holding up his glass for a refill. I clinked glasses with the part-time singer, then leaned over and kissed her firmly on the lips. It beat the champagne. She seemed to agree.

"We made it! We made it!" James Goldman was cheering lustily from the front of the cabin. He had commandeered what looked like a magnum of champagne and was spilling it freely.

"I say, John," said Thorne. "See if you can get some more of this stuff. Not the usual rotgut at all. Goldman has that whole bottle all to himself."

The steward, wreathed in smiles, spared me the trip, pouring out the Dom Perignon as though it were water. I was ready for seconds on kisses, too, and started to turn to my neighbor. Thorne diverted me, unhappily.

"Rowdy bunch on this plane," he said. "I'm all for revelry, mind you, and this champagne is truly superb. But what is it we're celebrating? Why is everyone shouting?''

I knew it. All those stories about Thorne sleeping through entire symphony concerts were God's truth. He had very nearly napped through a plane ditch. How to tell him? Where to begin?

"Why are all those planes escorting us?" he asked. "Why are there so many boats down below?"

I looked out the window and found that Thorne was right. While minimizing the crisis to us, the captain had apparently sent a Mayday alert to every vessel within a fifty-mile radius. From our low altitude, we could see the boat passengers waving their arms, T-shirts, semaphores, and—in one case—trousers, all to show their joy at our narrow escape.

"Maybe they heard you were coming, Sherrill."

Sherrill Thorne observed the scene, then modestly agreed. "You're probably right," he said. "The *Globe* must have sent down a press release about my coming."

I sighed deeply. Then suddenly, the seascape was replaced by landscape, land without hills. We were almost grazing the tops of the palm trees.

Then a runway came in sight, the tarmac covered with foam and dotted with fire trucks. Frightening sight. We waited for the ritual of the jolt of the landing gear as it locked into position. Instead, the plane circled in a wide arc.

My new acquaintance leaned across the aisle and tapped my arm.

"Did you hear the landing gear go down?" she asked.

"Why? Was it off-pitch?"

"You know what I mean. They can't get the landing gear down, or we would have heard it."

"Nonsense. Two crises in one day are out of the question. The collective heartbeat in this plane has simply drowned out the sound of the landing gear."

The captain's voice enveloped us again and sternly commanded us to lock our seatbelts and to place our heads down as we'd been shown earlier.

I locked up my ravishing neighbor, pushed her head down, then turned to show Thorne the crash position. Complaining that "they never make you do this foolishness on TWA," Thorne was all for gossip while curling up like a fetus.

"That's the girl!" he whispered.

"I know that! Keep your head down! She's singing with us. If we make it. Now shut up, Sherrill."

At that moment, the plane's belly touched the ground. We felt the skidding as the fuselage ricocheted down the foamed runway. For one perilous moment, it seemed that the whole aircraft was going to fall apart. Somehow it didn't. Somehow the plane came in straight as an arrow, its nose aloft and its wings level. A virtuoso performance. The masterpiece of belly landings. What a pilot.

I grabbed Ms. Hasse by one arm and Thorne by the other and pushed them through the emergency chute closest to us. Someone from behind pushed me.

In seconds, we were safely through. Passengers plopped out of the chute like change from a cigarette vendor. Goldman held on to his violin as if it were his firstborn. Rheinwein got through and promptly ran his hands over the frame of his cello, much as a surgeon would check a body for tumors.

I looked around for Thorne and, uh, what's-her-name—Hedda Hasse—but I couldn't see anything but hordes of newsmen, television cameras, and flashing camera bulbs.

Then the crowds thinned slightly, and I saw Ms. Hasse talking to a wraith of a man with a jaunty sports cap on his head. He was holding her firmly by the waist, and on his face was the beatific look you often see on the faces of fifteen-year-olds in the first stages of puppy love. Not often do you see it, though, on the mugs of septuagenarians. Though he was older and thinner—emaciated, in fact—than the last time I'd seen him, I recognized Antonio Saul Yera. To my surprise, he smiled to me in recognition and welcome.

"John Field, isn't it? It must be a decade since we performed together in Paris. How good to see you again. And safe—after that terrible journey. Hedda, I left your car at Harmonia and brought the heli over. Can I give you a ride there, Mr. Field? Or have you had enough air travel for one day?"

Had I had enough air travel for one day. Not even a shiny private helicopter and the close proximity of a lovely damsel could lure me off solid land that particular afternoon. I gave thanks and apologies to them both and made vague noises about renting a car.

"Oh, you won't need a car on Key Cohen," said Yera.

"Everybody walks over there. My chauffeur is bringing the limousine around now for those of you who don't wish to fly. It will take a little longer by ferry, but I'm afraid that's the only way to get there."

"Ferry?" I floundered. "Is Harmonia on an island or something?"

Yera looked at me patiently. "*Key* means island, Mr. Field. Cohen was my maternal grandfather's name. He bought the island and named it after himself. I built Harmonia and named it after my guiding muse. Here comes my driver. He'll see to you—and I'll meet you over at Harmonia."

A mammoth gray limousine drove up, and a matching gray driver (gray hair, gray uniform, gray face) emerged as if from a tomb. Yera addressed him in Spanish and, with that, departed in a whirl of dust with Hedda.

No sooner had they gone than Sherrill Thorne appeared at my side, baggage intact and in hand. More than I could say for my black bag. Though I'd rather it were in the sea than me.

"Was that Antonio Yera?" he asked.

"In the flesh."

"And he left with that beauty you introduced me to? I told you! That's the girl!"

"Must I always be your straight man? All right then, *what* girl, Mr. Interlocutor?"

"Wife Number Six. To be. Or is it Five? He's mad about her, you know. His works are laced with allusions to a Hedda. And that's our Hedda. They say she's been his creative inspiration."

"They?" I asked.

"Critics," he amplified.

"Oh, well, as long as *they* say so. One is hard pressed to keep up with critics' latest disclosures on the creative source of genius. Today, a beautiful woman. Tomorrow, a bowl of soup."

Eight passengers, you'll agree, should fill up all the space in any given limousine. Not this one. This one was so obscenely gigantic that we all had ample legroom.

"Comfortable," said James Goldman, "but not the type of vehicle that I'd take joy-riding."

"It could always double as a hearse," suggested Seamus Connacht.

"It will, too," added Ted Holzman, "if all those rumors about Yera are true."

"Oh, they're true all right." Thorne plopped into the conversation. "He's a dying man."

"He doesn't act like a dying man," I said. "You told me, Sherrill, that he's planning to marry again. Is that the action of a dying man?"

"Let's just say that it's the action of a man who intends to die happy. But you talked to him. What did you think?"

"He's paper thin," I admitted. "But his color is good. Besides, he's been composing up a storm, as we all know. Why does everyone insist he's dying?"

"He's had far too many hospitalizations lately," said Thorne, adjusting a cuff link inscribed with a sharp sign. "Word always gets out about those, and the press releases are so vague, you know he's sick."

"Cancer, you think?" asked Goldman.

Thorne shrugged his shoulders. "What else? I wonder who'll get that enormous fortune?"

"His current wife, I imagine."

I pointed out to Goldman that his suggestion would not hold water, since the composer was not presently married.

"As Mark Twain said, 'If you don't like the weather, wait a minute,' " replied the violinist. "Antonio Yera must say that about wives."

Thorne objected to the remark, implying as it did that his idol had feet of clay. I objected to it, too, for reasons clear only to my subconscious mind. We both glowered at him, but Goldman was much too busy looking out the windows to notice.

"We're getting on a boat!" he said. "Ferry of some sort. Why are we getting on a boat?"

Panic broke out in the car with this announcement.

There was, I explained, no cause for alarm. A ferry was the only way to reach Key Cohen. Harmonia was situated on Key Cohen. It was all crystal clear to me. Why not to them? It dawned on me finally that not one of the group welcomed me as a traveling companion. Anyplace.

All things considered, though, the boat ride over was quite

uneventful. Admittedly, a truck broke loose from its moorings, dumping lumber all over the surrounding cars. (All but ours.) True, the ship yawed and jawed quite alarmingly until the runaway truck was fastened down again. I will even own to some tense minutes when the boatswain brought lifejackets and issued hurried instructions on how to abandon ship.

But aside from the above, no problems. None at all.

For the life of me, I can't understand why Rheinwein felt compelled to tell me at one point that he wished to be buried with his cello but not here and not now. Or why Connacht had to be helped from the car, once we reached our destination.

5

THE thought had occurred to me—somewhere in the middle of our short voyage—that all of us on that ferry were going to the same place. That the boat had only one destination—Key Cohen. That every passenger present, excepting ourselves, was dressed for a gala performance of some sort. That such a performance would inevitably be—

Ours.

The cold feeling in the pit of my stomach rapidly spread to my arms, legs, and fingers. I didn't dare bring up this prospect to my colleagues for fear of being blamed for it. So I decided to let them figure it out for themselves.

Nicholas Rouse was the first one to piece the puzzle together. Once we arrived at Harmonia, he unwound his long body from the gray limousine and said to me, "See that woman in the sable wrap? Over there, near the portico?"

I agreed a fur was tasteless, in this heat, but my reply did not deflect him.

"She was on the ferry, too," he said. "She wanted my life preserver for her sable. You don't suppose our *audience* was on that ferry?

"You don't suppose," he continued in a sepulchral tone, "they haven't canceled tonight's performance?"

"Impossible," said Sherrill Thorne. "Although I have always called Floridians the only American aborigines, I'm sure they possess the rudiments of good manners. No musician could be expected to perform after the rigors of this afternoon. Let me see if I can't talk to Antonio about this. Do you see him? Surely we're jumping to conclusions.''

We all looked, but Yera was nowhere to be seen. Nor was the estimable Ms. Hasse. Reassuring when you considered that the performance could not take place if the pivotal singer was missing. Not so reassuring, to my mind, when you considered the number of bedrooms available for frolicking in a mansion this size.

How big was this size? Let's just say that Harmonia was a perfect match for the limousine that brought us here. Enormous, vulgar, tasteless—it had all the ingredients for success except moderation. Surprising, too, because the lines of the building were as classic as those of Versailles. The architect had known what he was doing; the decorator hadn't. Not with those gaudy awnings detracting attention from the arched symmetry of the windows. Not with the heavy-handed landscaping erasing the impact of the stately royal palms near the entrance gate. Not with—but you get the idea. Overdone.

We had drifted over toward the colonnades framing the entrance. In our wrinkled suits and rumpled neckties, we were a sorry-looking lot, clearly out of place among the peacocks in their assorted finery. Little did these birds know that we were what they had paid so handsomely to hear.

Someone must have spotted us, for in no time at all a servant emerged from the mansion's interior and ushered us to a courtyard. And to what appeared to be a receiving line.

For us? Apparently.

A tall, faded blonde in draped and flowing red silk stood at the head of the column and steered each of us down the line, delivering an identical opening remark: ''Ah'm Connie Weber, chaihman of the Ahts Committee, and you must be—''

She then registered a total lack of recognition as one face after another, all familiar figures on the international concert scene, filed past her.

Her next sentence touched briefly on commiseration and went along these lines: ''Ah just know you'll wanna rest up aftuh that ordeal, but you'll have plenty of time to do that while we're partyin'. The performance isn't for two hours yet. Fuhst, though, ah'd like ya to meet the sponsors of ouah fine festival.''

"May I present"—she went on—"Consul Armando Argento. From Salvanigua—" I touched the clammy hand of the aging diplomat and gazed into a fleshy face studded by small, beady eyes. "Short and fat" about describes him.

"—and his charming wife Alicia—" But not her. She was, to use the vernacular, a knockout. Black hair drawn back dramatically from an oval, burnished face. Barely thirty, with a petite but deep, shall we say, décolletage. The eyes plunged—involuntarily—down, down that neckline. I greeted her warmly.

"Have we met, Meester Field?" I noticed her spouse's suspicious glance.

"Ah," I sighed, kissing her hand, "those nights in Venice!"

She looked at me in some puzzlement and passed me along down the line, as one would a hot potato.

Connie, wafted in aroma, hauled me bodily to the next line.

"—Mr. and Mrs. Radler, true bastions of the arts here in Fun City. Dick Radler is president of the Offshore Banking Corporation and his wife Rachael is the community's guiding impresario—and her spouse's support and mainstay, it goes without saying."

It goes *with* saying that Rachael was built like a fullback gone to fat and that her support was the only thing keeping her spouse upright right now. Dick murmured pleasantries in a drunken slur, while I noted the jaundiced pallor and the thin frame of the confirmed alcoholic.

"—Bob O'Reilly, one of the city's leading attorneys and by far the handsomest of the lot." O'Reilly did not deny the charge. The features were almost too good to be true—and here and there, I saw the telltale lines of the plastic surgeon's scalpel. Blond hair. Dark roots. Fairly tall. He passed me along without a word pro or con.

"General Vance Sweeten," continued Ms. Weber, "one of the great military minds of World War Two." She leaned over and planted a juicy one on the great mind's face. "I'm sure you know the name." I did—but not the face. Forty summers between then and now had furrowed the brow recorded in history books. Worse yet, the general's sight was nearly gone now, judging from the thickness of the glasses perched on the nose. The nose, meanwhile, was sniffing the night air, while the mouth was complaining loudly about "pollution smells everywhere."

"I admire your work," he said, looking straight at the fountain. I gazed back into the fat lenses—very much like looking into the reverse end of a telescope—and thanked him.

"—and his vivacious wife, Frieda," Connie Weber went on. The original wife, one would surmise, since she was equally aged and worn as the general. Oblivious to the blow Time had dealt her, she was gadded out, here and there, in emerald green satin and topped off with a sparkling tiara on all-too-red hair. Frieda placed a withered talon on my arm and guided me to the bulldog next to her.

"Lorenzo DaPonto," Connie droned on, "our able police commissioner." This bulldog smoked cigars and failed to remove the stogie now implanted between his lips. "Helluva trip down, wasn't it!" The lips expanded into a smile but never loosed their hold on the cigar. "This is my wife, Lisa, by the way."

Lisa, I felt sure, was always "by the way." If long-suffering could be personified, Lisa would fill the bill. Definitely hangdog, I thought. But why? All the trappings of wealth enveloped her—as with all the others—but here they created a fantasy world. Pink tulle, by the acre, seemed to me like an echo from the past. That and the trapped eyes in a haggard face. Dark eyes, dusky complexion. Latin, surely, like her husband.

We came to the end of the line, where the chairman introduced me to a muscular, swarthy, hostile specimen of Hispanic male. In appearance, a light heavyweight. Early thirties.

"Mr. Miguel Ochelly," she stated, as if that explained all. I waited for the expected sobriquet. Ex-pugilist? Chauffeur? Drug runner? All of the above?

Ms. Weber placed a proprietary arm on the bulging left forcep of Ochelly and added, "Miguel's from Colombia and doesn't know a lot of English. He's been wonderfully generous, though, to our fund-raising efforts for the center. Like the rest of the patrons you've just met, he's contributed more than $300,000 to—oh, there you are, Joseph! You're late!

"Mr. Field," she continued, "may I present another artist like yourself—Joseph Lange, the renowned earth painter."

I looked closely at the man whose lunacy was legendary. Older than I expected—probably late fifties. A huge head set on a small body. On the head, masses of gray hair that joined forces with a beard at about chin level. Evasive eyes that lit on you briefly, then flew off at a tangent. You probably remember that, among his many exploits, he dressed the Statue of Liberty in a tutu some years back. Then there was the notorious episode at Norma's Vineyard. . . .

Connie Weber interrupted these musings with the suggestion that we adjourn to the bar. I noticed that the reception line had broken up and that a great many people were milling about the courtyard now—most of them gravitating toward the buffet table opposite us. Food, above all, was what I needed and where my nose led me. But Ms. Weber slipped one hand through Ochelly's arm and the other through mine and guided us farther down the courtyard.

"What you really need after that unnerving experience," she said, "is a good, stiff drink! The show must go on, I know, but—"

"Why?" I asked sensibly.

"Well, we know that the last thing musicians would ever want to do is cancel a performance and—"

"Nonsense," I said. "It happens all the time. Performances are canceled constantly every day of the week. Rain, snow, sleet—lack of money, half the time. Surely a near-crash offers enough reason for postponing the performance until tomorrow. A traumatic experience like that is bound to affect our—"

"Do you want some Jack Daniel's?" she interrupted. "Surely that will take care of a little case of nerves."

I summoned up all the hauteur at my disposal. "I never drink before a performance, and I never have a case of nerves, little or big. Postponing just seems to me the only rational thing to do. Good form, you know."

"Good form?" The chairperson of the board lolled the words around in her mouth, then spat them out. Unpalatable.

"We took a vote, you know. But since several of the board members are scheduled to leave for a safari this week, they just thought . . . well, it was so late to cancel, you know. We just thought y'all would want . . . well, I'm sure you understand, Mr. Field."

The fact was that I understood all too well. We'd been carted down here, we had accepted handsome fees, we would play. I got the distinct impression that the performance would have taken place even if the plane had ditched with all hands lost. Even if the members of the board had had to substitute for the musicians. Even if they had had to learn to read music first.

Why the urgency?

At that moment, Sherrill Thorne approached us, as bubbly as the champagne he carried. A retinue followed. First, the luscious Madame Argento, hovered over by the watchful Argento. Then Rachael Radler, sans spouse—where could he be?—and Frieda Sweeten, who bluntly explained that her husband abhorred large gatherings and was listening to his host's record collection.

"What are you going to do now, John?" asked Thorne.

"Do?" Rachael Radler jumped in the conversational swim. "Do about what?"

"John's lost all his baggage—clothes, music, everything. That will teach you to check things through, John. I stopped doing that years ago."

Mrs. Radler took one long, searching look at my ragged beard and my unkempt clothes and decided that something had to be done—and quickly.

"How tall are you?" she asked. "Five foot nine—something like that?"

"Five foot ten," I replied, stretching it a bit.

"That's about Tony's height. And he is—or was—just about your build, too. The build of a Spanish dancer. I'm sure he'll have a tuxedo around that he can lend you for the evening."

"And the music?" Thorne was relentless.

"Well, surely he has the original manuscript here somewhere. Where else would it be? I'll go find him. He really should be out here with his guests."

"Maybe he's resting," suggested Thorne.

"No, he's not," said Frieda Sweeten. "He's listening to records with Vance. Downright rude, if you ask me, but you don't teach an old dog new tricks." She failed to distinguish between old dogs, so I assumed she meant her husband. After a time, I've noticed, wives give up on apologizing for the social shortcomings of their mates. Or any other shortcomings, either.

Busy as I was wolfing down food, I did notice that the shades of evening were falling rather steadily, and I knew the buffet table would have to be abandoned any minute now.

"Could anyone tell me," I managed between morsels, "where to go from here?"

"I could, John," replied Thorne. "Or did you mean—where is your room?"

Connie Weber was anxious to help. "I think you and Mr. Thorne are staying in the South Tower rooms." She pointed vaguely beyond the open gallery overlooking the courtyard.

"I can't see them," said Thorne, following the pointed finger. "Oh, you mean higher yet. My, that is a tower!"

I glanced heavenward and finally spotted a trinity of windows, two of them opening to a common balcony. Awfully high up.

"You're on the left, Mr. Thorne," said Connie.

"Oh, that's the Madame de Pompadour Room!" squealed Alicia. "Such privacy, such a view—"

"Such a lot of steps," I added lamely.

"Music, music everywhere," enthused Thorne. "Look at that magnificent grillwork!" He pointed to the crossbars, slightly askew, on all the windows.

Alicia continued her commentary. "The rooms are narrow, but they run the width of the entire wing. You'll look out the bay on the opposite side."

Connie couldn't wait until I did just that. She consulted, rather pointedly, a diamond-studded wristwatch and asked, "Had enough to eat, Mr. Field? Maybe I can send up a doggie bag. I'll have the butler escort you up to your rooms—and I'll check on that tuxedo, too."

With that, the elegant Amazon swept off, while I searched out Thorne, though still smarting under the doggie-bag crack. Entirely uncalled for, if you ask me.

But Thorne begged off on the journey upward, insisting that anyone who could find his way in and out of the *New York Globe* would be undeterred by the labyrinthine ways of Harmonia. Besides, he was having far too good a time to leave now, and he was soaking up atmosphere for a truly exhaustive description of the Master's house in that forthcoming biography.

"Did you see that inscription by the fountain?" He dragged me to the center of the courtyard for a closer look. "Another tribute to his new girlfriend."

"I see water spilling over shapeless blocks of black stone. That's a tribute?"

"Abstract expressionism at its bleakest, I agree," said Thorne. "But the words are clear enough. See, there's a message spelled in mosaic on the courtyard tiles—'Music As Thy Name Is.' Beautiful, isn't it?"

"Francis Thompson probably thought so. It's his poem. That hardly names names, Sherrill. Besides, the sculpture looks new, and the inscription is old and worn. If this is even remotely connected with that girl on the plane, the significance is lost on me."

"But don't you see?" Thorne asked. "Music *as thy name is*. It's a clue to the music. It's like a treasure hunt with messages planted in odd places—"

"Impossible. That sculpture is the work of a sick mind."

"The sculpture, yes, but everything here is a love letter in the sands, so to speak—"

A butler, imposing in his bulk, cleared his throat to draw our attention. One does not ignore two hundred fifty pounds of beef on the hoof, so I followed obediently in his steps.

We crossed the courtyard and climbed a spacious set of marble steps to the gallery balcony. Then we circled the gallery and took a narrower coral staircase opening from this second level. Finally, we entered the last lap by means of a perpendicular spiral staircase leading to a small hallway. Each set of stairs was darker than the last, culminating in this inner sanctum illuminated by a shaded table lamp. The butler opened the door to the right of the landing, and I buzzed on through—straight to the balcony, where I stood and gulped large mouthfuls of fresh air. Huffing and puffing I was. How would a man of Sherrill's age make that ascent later on?

"Next time," suggested the butler with a discreet sneer, "perhaps you'd prefer to take the elevator."

"Elevator!"

"Yes, sir, just over this way." He pointed toward the opposite end of the hallway. "I think you'll find it small but efficient."

I looked for something to brandish, but he had disappeared.

Silent as a cat.

6

THE ladies were as good as their word. My borrowed
tuxedo—with all accessories—lay neatly placed out on
my bed, and I could see at a glance that it would fit.

Since the bed was laden with clothes, forty winks was out
of the question. So I stepped out on the balcony again and
looked down on the hordes below. Snatches of dialogue
drifted upward, disembodied remarks from unidentified
speakers.

"Fantastic tax shelter . . ."

"You can deduct your mother-in-law . . ."

"With double depreciation, you say?"

". . . too dangerous now . . . later. . . ."

This last uttered in low but carrying tones. Another tax
hedge, no doubt, but still . . .

A quick glance at my watch (not diamond-encrusted) convinced me that time was of the essence all right. So I shaved
and showered quickly, then donned Yera's old tuxedo. The
cut was old-fashioned, but then, the suit was old. I found half
a ticket stub from some long-forgotten concert in one of the
pockets. Then I looked at myself in the full-length mirror of
the armoire. Perfect. Even the cummerbund fit. I was feeling
better by the minute. Now for the music—

A knock at the door solved that problem. Antonio Saul

Yera himself stood on the landing, manuscript in hand and worry apparent on his thin face. He came straight to the point.

"You will be careful of these pages, won't you?" he asked. "They're already willed to the Smithsonian. Tick-tack-toe scribblings and all."

"I will treat them like the gold, incense, and myrrh they are. I promise. Thank you so much for lending them."

He stepped inside and surveyed the surroundings.

"You like your room?"

For the first time, I looked at it and rendered judgment.

"It's sumptuous," I said. "Even Madame de Pompadour would have been pleased with it."

"That's said to be her bed, you know. All the other pieces are Italian."

"Oh, that explains all the wood inlays. I was beginning to think Louis XV's mistress was musical." Yera looked quizzical. "The sharp signs, I mean."

"I'd forgotten," said Yera. "I haven't been up here in years."

Oh. The suspicion dawned that another mistress might have occupied this room and that the choice of bed was indeed apropos. None of my business. I flipped hurriedly through the manuscript in an attempt to change the subject.

"Would you mind if I showed this to Sherrill Thorne? He'd be as honored as I to examine it."

"I don't think we'll have time before the performance—"

"Afterward, of course. We're pressed for time as it is."

"Can you point out Thorne to me from here? We've never met, you know."

We stepped out on the small balcony overlooking the courtyard. The scent of gardenias wafted upward along with the murmur of the crowd below us. From the tops of the assembled heads, I spied Thorne's naked skull next to the flourishing scalp of Luciano Lacramose. Our conductor for the evening was boasting to Thorne that he never used a score on the podium—"I always conduct from memory, always"— and was expounding to the critic, a man who knew better, that "Johann Strauss, Jr., was the greatest composer who ever lived." Thorne responded by blowing smoke in his face. I pointed out the critic to Yera.

"I should be able to recognize someone with whom I have

so much in common. Thorne is as bald as I am." He turned back inside, muttering, "We'd better hurry, Mr. Field."

I trotted after Antonio Yera, who moved quickly for an old man. We took an elevator and various back corridors that led through the mansion's interior and onto a secluded terrace, surrounded by a cluster of magnolia trees.

"I'm taking you in the back way," explained Yera. "Through the boxholders' private terrace."

He unlatched a heavy wooden door that opened onto a small vestibule.

"The door on the left leads backstage," he said. "And the stairway goes to the private boxes upstairs. But before you go backstage, let me show you the Hall of Mirrors from the audience's perspective."

He opened the arched door directly in front of us onto the broad back of a security guard. The guard turned to face us and hastily amended his hostile frown to a smile of welcome.

"Ah, jit's you, sir," he said in the soft Spanish accent that so tenderly mangles English. He moved aside to let us pass.

"Expecting trouble?" I asked Yera.

"Not really. But with all the drug crime down here, people are nervous about being out after dark. This is just a little extra precaution for our board members. The women will all be wearing their jewels tonight."

"But isn't the guard in the wrong place?"

"What do you mean?"

"The boxholders will be perfectly safe from the audience downstairs. But wouldn't they be, anyway? I believe I read in the *Sun* that everyone invited to this evening's performance had given at least $100,000 to the arts center."

"Money doesn't make for respectability, Mr. Field."

"That's true. But while you're protecting the balcony from the audience inside, who is to protect them from the enemy outside? Who knows what evil lurks—"

Yera laughed off my dramatics. "Oh, there's a guard on the terrace right now. He'll stay until the boxholders go upstairs and lock this door then. Come look around."

The Hall of Mirrors was all that and more. A crazyhouse of mirrors. Mirrors everyplace. On the walls. On the ceiling. Mirrors set at every angle. Mirrors on the stage. In the auditorium. On the balcony. Only there was the effect softened by rich red draperies draping the sides of each box and by touches of matching fabric wallcoverings.

Whoever had designed this hall had seen the Hall of Mirrors at Versailles. But he had gone about twenty steps too far from that architectural achievement. Good taste had been replaced by excess.

"Magnificent, isn't it?" Yera interrupted my thoughts.

"Has it always been like this?"

"Not at all. I've just had Joseph Lange redo it, as a matter of fact. You've heard of him? This is one of his first commissions in architectural design. His most spectacular successes have been in environmental paintings."

Something snapped in place.

"Norma's Vineyard," I said. "And New York, too."

"Great achievements—appreciated only by the most discerning."

"Will Joseph Lange be coming to tonight's performance?"

"Of course. Tonight will be the dedication of his new theater as part of the arts center. We'd better be going backstage now. The other musicians are already there."

Yera ushered me back through the golden arches to the stage door and—with ardent wishes to "break a leg"—left me there.

Five minutes to liftoff.

"He's here!" cried James Goldman.

Eight faces turned toward me with expressions mingling anger, fear, and relief.

"How grand of you not to wait till the last minute," said Seamus Connacht. His silver flute was perched on his lips, and he went right on warming up on scales in all keys. Everyone considered this sufficient rebuke and resumed the cacophony that signals the performance is about to begin.

Seconds later, Ted Holzman carefully set down his clarinet and peered through the stage door.

"They're all out there," he said, "and they're dimming the lights in the hall. We're on! You lead the way, Ms. Hasse."

With no sign of a limp at all, Hedda Hasse marched onstage. She looked spectacular in a long, ice-blue gown that heightened the blue of her eyes and concealed the white of her cast. (It also obeyed Chanel's maxim: "Less is more.") She walked as though she were going to be crowned Queen of England at the opposite side of the stage.

The rest of us shambled in as musicians do. That is, we leaped, lurked, and lurched toward our destinations, bumping instruments and music stands along the way. In our tuxedoes of varying ages and designs, we looked like seven bridegrooms on a wedding cake with Hedda Hasse the one radiant bride.

A sprinkling of applause greeted us. We bowed in unison and in dignity—as though the rafters were being torn down by the audience's sheer joy at seeing us.

I sat at a magnificent gold Steinway that—to the naked eye—had all its keys intact. I covertly glanced through the piano's open lid and noted that the strings were not conspicuous by their absence. Handsome Hedda Hasse stood to my left. She inched forward until our sightlines were established and we could communicate with head nods. The remaining musicians grouped themselves into a semicircle where I could see them and they could see me. So far, so good.

All were present and accounted for except our conductor, who dawdled in the wings. Ostensibly, he was waiting until the instruments were tuned and ready to go. Actually, he was delaying his entrance until the contralto's effect had abated slightly. Or so I suspected.

As I began to place the score on the piano, a wisp of a youth appeared at my elbow and announced, "I am your page-turner."

From the width of his glasses and the drone of his speech, I would guess he had more than a nodding acquaintance with computers. Still, I welcomed his reassuring presence and told him to pull up a chair. The manuscript, though Holy Writ, was a mass of unstapled pages. Yera had assured me that the pages were all in precise order. I checked through the music hurriedly. Yes, all was in order.

Then Goldman asked for an A on the piano (for the obligatory tuning of instruments), and I obligingly struck out an A.

Only it was not an A.

It was a G.

The piano was a full tone flat.

The violinist looked at me, aghast. The contralto's lovely mouth flew open. A frightened buzz went through the assorted musicians. In that moment of terror, I took my thumb and ran it the entire length of the keyboard. All eighty-eight keys showed no liabilities other than that single damning one: the piano was a full tone off-pitch.

"What are we going to do?" Goldman's voice was soft—it is always soft in a crisis. I barely heard him.

"We're going to play it."

"How can we play it? You're a full tone flat. It will sound like a band playing 'The Star Spangled Banner' in two different keys. Even those dolts out there will know something's wrong."

"Goldy, we're going to play it. I'll transcribe my part up."

"That's impossible. Brahms was the last musician who could do a thing like that."

"I know the music. I'll manage."

To look at the violinist's face, you'd think we were facing a greater crisis than we had on the plane. And in a sense, we were: Every time a musician plays, he puts his life—his musical life and reputation—on the line.

No time for more reassuring words to Goldy, though. Luciano Lacramose chose that moment to sweep out on the stage. Had the twit been listening, he would have had the good sense to hide under the closest bench. But no. In white tie and tails, he burst upon our little tableau like a Christ figure.

Serenely confident, Lacramose beamed and bowed to the audience, then turned to us. With a look that blended condescension with arrogance in equal measure, he lifted his baton and his eyebrows and his expectations.

Obviously, he hadn't heard my A.

Down came the baton. And we were off.

7

THE woodwinds and strings begin the Concerto with a lyrical passage and carry on in gorgeous fashion for fifty measures or so. I moved my eyes ahead to the measure where I would enter. My solo started simply enough with ten exquisite chords,* and I had ample time to enjoy the music before joining in.

But wait! Something was going drastically wrong with the performance. I looked at the conductor. His arms were flailing about all right, but nothing they were doing corresponded to what the instruments were doing.

I checked the score: The Concerto begins in quarter time—four beats to a measure with deceptively simple passages—then switches to increasingly complex rhythms as the parts begin to subdivide. At some points, two and three different pulses emerge from the mosaic of the orchestral tapestry while the music grows in intensity. For this work, two conductors are really needed, though the composer asks for only one. A

---

* Some of the chordal notes had been set forth in red in the manuscript: B, E, two repeated D's, A. Then B, A, E flat, another E flat echoing an octave higher and melting into E natural. For the first time, I realized these notes, surrounded and embellished by their glorious harmonies, formed the core of the work.

gifted one, preferably, but one who can in any event beat time. Anyone, in short, but Luciano Lacramose.

With a shock of enlightenment, I realized what was happening. He was conducting from memory, and he was conducting in waltz time! Three beats to the measure and probably ''Wienerblut,'' judging from his ecstatic expression.*

Somebody had to do something. The winds were doing their best to ignore Lacramose, but direction was clearly needed as the parts multiplied and divided. And I was the only one onstage with the full score.

So I did something. I raised my hands high above the keyboard, eyed every one of the musicians, and jiggled my shoulders to clearly indicate: ''Watch me.''

Then I came in with my solo, transposed my chords a full step upward, and cued in Hedda with my chin. She repeated the ten-note theme while the piano embroidered arabesques above, over, and around her. I hardly noticed how she sounded, so pleased was I that she'd caught my cue. Goldy caught on immediately. He was instantly in perfect synchronization with Hedda and me. But for a space of several measures, only we three kept the performance together.

For a while there, it was Tinker to Evers to Chance.

Then everybody grabbed the brass ring, and we began settling down to the performance of our lives. It was ensemble playing of the highest order—one of those rare moments when musicians become the invisible channels between the composer and the listener. The clear, glass vessel that serves up the alchemy.

At this point, my hands were playing music of enormous difficulty and were transposing the notes a full step upward from the thickets of the score. My head was bobbing up and down to indicate pulse and changes of meter to the other musicians. My chin was cueing in every entrance. My shoulders were conducting the entire ensemble.

And it was working! Lacramose had been neutralized, and the performance was taking off on its own set of wings. I darted a glance up toward the boxes to see how the composer

* *That* was what he had meant by that irrelevant remark to Thorne in the courtyard.

was taking this incredible music-making. There he sat, impassive and detached as a toad. Out of the corner of my eye, I saw Thorne's reflection. The critic looked thunderstruck. One person, at least, who appreciated what he was hearing.

A shadow fell across my music as we neared the end of a page. I whispered to the page-turner to get out of the light and to turn the page, which I had been doing up to now.

He seemed transfixed. Terrified.

"Turn the page," I hissed, in a voice that must have carried to the back row.

"No!" He was even more forceful.

No? *No?* This refugee from a robot factory was telling me *no?* If my hands hadn't been all tied up at the time, I'd have used them to kill the page-turner. So God punished me for bad intentions by wafting up the stack of unstapled pages on a draft of warm air.

This was turning into a Perils of Pauline. All that saved me now was that the piano had a rest for a few measures, giving me time to leap for the music. With an athletic grace directly attributable to my staying in shape at all times, I caught the pages as they trickled down from on high. The right one first. What a break.

I came in again, right on time, for my next solo. It was like a no-hit, no-run game. No one wants to admit it's perfect for fear of spoiling the spell. But it was perfect. In spite of everything, this performance was turning into a monumental one. Incapable of nothing less than greatness.

So I couldn't believe what I heard next—and from no less a listener than Sherrill Thorne.

"Careless!" he said. Right out loud. Loud enough for everyone to hear. Loud enough for *us* to hear.

How could he do this? All right—my spilling of pages, that was careless but understandable. To condemn us all—that was like taking hostages and shooting the children. I had been clumsy. No one else.

I went on playing. We all did, seemingly unperturbed. Then the music diminished to a point of absolute stillness. A dramatic silence that seemed carved out of eternity itself.

All alone, rising out of the silence, Hedda began to sing.

Alone, the contralto sang the ten notes of the theme, but this time, words etched out the pain implicit in the music:

> Naked and alone
>   we came into exile . . .*

Her voice burst forth like a wellspring. Clear and flowing and so artless that it was the height of art. Mahogany tones—deep and burnished and somber. All invested with such natural musicality that I realized the truth of what I never quite admitted before: that every instrument—even the piano—is but an imitation of the voice. And ultimately, every instrument pales beside it.

The unaccompanied chant went on:

> O waste of loss, in the hot mazes,
>   lost, among bright stars
>   on this most weary unbright cinder,
>   lost!

We were all listening to her, and I thought I detected tears on the cheeks of the nerveless Goldman. There was a lump in my own throat that was very hard to explain. I collected myself in time to come in on the words,

> Remembering speechlessly we seek
>   the great forgotten language,
>   the lost lane-end into heaven,
>   a stone, a leaf, an unfound door.

With the entrance of the clarinet, the duo metamorphosed—almost mystically—into a trio. Then all the musicians joined the singer in a climax of sound on the phrase,

> O lost, and by the wind grieved, ghost,
>   come back again.

* Thomas Wolfe, excerpted from *Look Homeward, Angel.* Copyright 1929 Charles Scribner's Sons; copyright renewed © 1957 Edward C. Aswell, Administrator, C.T.A. and/or Fred W. Wolfe. Reprinted with the permission of Charles Scribner's Sons.

Here the work sheds all pretense on its origins—as sensually and as directly as a woman sheds her clothes to make love. It quotes directly from the closing passages of the "Art of the Fugue" by Johann Sebastian Bach. Why on earth hadn't I noticed that before?

Now I could see it—plain as day—on the manuscript in front of me. The repeated notes of the theme become woven into the counterpoint of Bach's name.* Asserting those notes, the contralto sings a vocal line that soars above the ensemble. Free as a comet. Yet shaded and balanced against the mass and timbres of the orchestral instruments.

The pianist, meanwhile, quotes the Bach passages—exactly as written in 1750 and with the same strict metrical requirements. And against these independent lines, the ensemble plays music that has shed its bar lines and its inhibitions and goes soaring away like a spaceship into the stars.

None of this is easy to bring off. But when it is done well, the beauty of the score surpasses and transforms all its difficulties. Tonight, we were playing with a deep, instinctive understanding of the music. I was grateful for the microphones and cameras recording this historic performance.

Suddenly, it was over. The composition ends like an apocalyptic vision. As abruptly as Bach's.

Like the moment of death.

---

* The Bach work breaks off—abruptly, decisively, irrevocably—with one of the most disturbing passages in all music. In musical counterpoint, the score spells out the letters B-A-C-H (which translates to B flat, A, C, B natural in German musical script). No sooner had Bach set the last letter of his name than he was stricken with blindness—the harbinger of his death.

8

In the momentary stillness that followed the performance, someone whispered "Bravo." Whispered it, mind you, but we heard it as clearly as though it had been shouted from the housetops.

The applause, when it came, was like an anticlimax after that "Bravo." I could swear it had come from Thorne's box—Thorne, who never allowed himself even the luxury of a half-smile before he wrote his review.

We all bowed, conscious that we had earned this applause and gratified that the audience had some appreciation of what they'd heard tonight. Our ornamental conductor bowed, but modestly. He bowed to *us*—a gesture that convinced me there was hope for the lad yet. The page-turner slunk off in the shadows, where I trust he had the decency to hang himself. Only performers are entitled to stage fright.

With a good grace that astonished me, Lacramose kept bringing us out for bows, insisting that Hedda Hasse, James Goldman, and myself take several bows—individual and collective—and even joining in the applause. Let me tell you, it was a night to remember. Between bows, I managed to whisper to Hedda Hasse that she wasn't a singer, she was a musician. It was the highest praise I could think of.

Finally, Lacramose turned to Antonio Yera with a deep bow of homage. Several in the audience began calling out

"Composer!" Sherrill Thorne too was on his feet shouting "More! More!"

Slowly and falteringly, Yera came up to the stage. He bowed to the audience, then turned toward Thorne's box and bowed again. I could hear the critic's shouted praises—"Hooray! . . . More! . . . More!"—along with continuing jabs at me—"Careless!" At least he didn't throw tomatoes.

Yera grasped the musicians by the hands and kissed the contralto on both cheeks. Then he stood with us to acknowledge the applause. And the shouts. We took nine curtain calls in all. They just wouldn't quit.

At last, Yera held up both hands over his head—like a prizefighter who has just scored a knockout punch—and we left the stage.

For good this time.

"What are they waiting for? Do they really expect an encore?"

I put the questions to Antonio Saul Yera in the wings. The applause had died down, but nobody seemed to be leaving. As far as I could see, the composer was the only authority around who could comment on native behavior.

"Oh, you're new to Florida, aren't you? The audience is waiting for the football scores."

"The what?"

"Football scores. Fun City has a professional football team, you know."

"The Manatees. Something like that."

"The Sharks, actually. Fortunately for us, they're playing out of town tonight. Otherwise, there'd be no audience at all."

"They really take football that seriously down here?"

"Seriously? The world will end tomorrow if the Sharks lose tonight's game. I hope they don't, but for purely selfish motives."

"What do you mean? The audience might leave?"

"En masse. And now if you'll excuse me, I'm going to introduce myself to Thorne. I congratulate you again. I just wish I'd felt well enough to conduct—"

Me too, I thought, but did not say.

"—but you managed beautifully, even without a baton. You

should give some thought to conducting. Next step up, you know, and a natural move for a consummate musician.''

I swelled a little. Nice thing for him to say. I was about to add appropriate encomia about his music calling forth the best in me. But he was off before I could warn him. I wanted to tell the composer that Sherrill would not welcome a visit, even from him, at this time. Thorne would regard it—as he did all remarks during a performance—as an attempt to influence his review. Oh well, Yera would find that out soon enough for himself. Serve him right, too. Just punishment for not having that piano tuned.

We had come off the stage to the right wings, and the curtains had been drawn so the stagehands could prepare the setting for the *Farewell Symphony.* I observed their machinations—setting up candelabras and the like—and the prospect of hearing the *Farewell* in a Hall of Mirrors enticed me to stay. Exhausted though I was.

The stage door opened to the right vestibule, which was just as small as its opposite. This one was mobbed and open to the public, which streamed through a large archway to the lounges below. I fought my way through the thundering herds to the auditorium, where front-row chairs had been roped off for our ensemble. Like a crab crawling sideways, I crept toward one, dimly noting that a spotlight played on the stage and that someone filled that spotlight to the very brim.

To the outer reaches and beyond, one might say. There wasn't a spotlight going that could fully envelop the ample form of—what was her name?—oh, yes. Rachael Radler. Impresario.

Suspense was mounting, and she milked it to the utmost. First the scores of games played on the West Coast. Then the Midwest. Then the South.

The really important game—the one that would determine the playoffs, as I believe they're called—she was sitting on until last. If she was sitting on it, it was in good hands. So to speak.

The audience—most of it, anyway—stayed fully rooted to their seats while Rachael droned on. I surveyed the scene in the half-lit hall. In the balcony above, I could see Yera talking to Thorne, but I couldn't overhear a thing he was saying.

Normally, my hearing is excellent. The odds were against

me here, though. Eavesdropping from a distance of seventy feet while someone is bellowing out football scores is not an easy task. So I scooted my chair around on the tiled floor, aiming it for a point directly beneath Thorne's box. Who would notice?

The security guard, in point of fact. One tapped me on the shoulder.

"Sorree, sir, you cannot do that." He spoke with the soft voice so prevalent in Florida.

"But I can't see from there." Neither could I hear.

"Eet moos stay."

"I won't hurt the chair, you know. I'm driving very carefully."

"Notheeng can be moved here. Everytheeng moos stay the same. That is the condeetions."

"The conditions? Of what?"

"Of the geeft!"

Oh, well. Now I had it. Apparently, Yera had tied in his donation of Harmonia with some strict requirements. Not a bad idea, all in all, if he wanted his gift to Fun City to remain in the pristine condition in which it was deeded.

Just then, I heard Rachael Radler come to what was—for many—the high point in the evening.

"Pittsburgh Ironers—*six!*" she cried.

Excitement was abuilding in the Hall of Mirrors. You could cut the tension with a knife. Still she paused. Teasingly. Expectantly. Catcalls broke out. Whistles.

"Fun City Sharks—" she teetered, like a ballerina, on the balance of the sentence.

"Fun City Sharks," she repeated *"seven!!!"*

Hysteria. Pandemonium. Total madness.

Did I say we had applause? I was wrong. They must have been dusting off their hands at the time. This, now. *This* was applause! Deafening waves of it. Peal upon peal. Endless clapping. Lots of jumping, stomping, and chanting. "Fun City *Sharks!* Fun City *Sharks!*"

I fully expected a stampede, and so apparently did the management, for the lights went on rather quickly and Rachael Radler got off the stage just as fast.

People began filing out, but since only five minutes' intermission remained, I stayed put. And looked up again toward Thorne's box.

Yera had left, but people were coming in by the cartful. I recognized most of the board members as they filed in, though I noticed the old general and his wife remained seated in their own box next to Thorne's. The critic was standing and greeting each visitor with no trace of a smile on his face. So much for solitude. Normally, Thorne was scratching furiously in his notebook during this period, so that his review was half-written before he even left the performance.

Rachael Radler appeared in the box then, as only she could appear, followed closely by—to my surprise—Hedda Hasse. That was where she had gone off to. I was disappointed. Why else had I placed my program in the next seat but to save a place for her? It looked like Yera would have company in his box for the Haydn.

But no. The composer popped up right by *my* elbow, full of smiles and cheer.

"Is that seat taken, Mr. Field?"

I hesitated. "Well, I think Ms. Hasse—"

Goldy spoke up and offered Antonio Yera his place, and our whole crew stood and moved as one farther down the row.

"Enjoy your talk with Sherrill Thorne?" I asked.

"He was most complimentary. About the music. I tried to soften his review—about the falling pages, I mean"—my God, I thought, that's the *last* thing you should do—"but the board members began arriving, and we didn't have much time to talk."

"Why did they bother?" I posed the question just as Hedda Hasse appeared at my other elbow. "Hadn't they already met him?"

"Oh," said Yera, "he didn't go through the receiving line, you know. I think he headed straight for the bar."

"The real reason," inserted Hedda, "is that Fun City has never seen a New York critic here before. For us, it's an event."

"Surely," I began, "the living presence of the world's leading contemporary composer is event enough for anybody—" Flies—or bees—began buzzing near my head. I swatted at one. How hot the hall had suddenly become!

"The real event," oozed Yera, "was the debut of a great singer." A trickle of sweat trickled down the composer's temple, and he reached for a cloth to mop his brow.

"No doubt about that." I joined gladly in the compliments—"Kirsten Waglock will have to move over"—but I was stopped midstream by a sharp sting to the forehead.

"What's the matter?" Yera dropped his handkerchief and gazed at me in surprise.

"Monster bees, I think." The lights, signaling the end of intermission, were flickering and beginning to dim.

"Something hit me, too! I think I've lost an earring!"

Just then I felt a vicious sting near my eye, blinding me for an instant. Angered, I slapped the culprit this time and slipped him in my pocket. I opened my eyes to find both my companions still searching the floor. But I looked up as the chandeliers rose to the ceiling and all light died.

Not before I saw the mirrored image of Sherrill Thorne peering down into the Hall of Mirrors.

9

"I don't think those were bees" muttered Hedda, two seats down.

"Opening the doors lets in all the heat and bugs," explained Yera. To the air, not to her, since the singer had risen and abruptly departed.

"Where is Hedda going?"

"I think she went over there"—Yera pointed vaguely toward the right—"to look for her earring. She'll be right back."

We were in that breathless frame of silence that surrounds every performance. Somebody coughed. A few rustled their programs. An epidemic of coughing began as the audience waited for the conductor to appear. A sprinkling of lights, as the art lovers checked their programs.

"Damn!" said Yera. "They'll spoil the effect. What's keeping the—"

"There *is* no conductor for the Haydn," I reminded him.

"Maybe the stagehand doesn't know that. I'll go up."

He shuffled off toward the open steps at our left. And like magic, the curtains parted a few seconds later to reveal a magical sight.

It was breathtaking. Now the full effect of the Hall of Mirrors enveloped us. The source of light was minimal—just two tiered chandeliers on marble tables flanking the small orchestra. Those and a single candle on each musician's music stand.

But that was all that was needed. The stage was bathed in light from the repeated images in the angled mirrors. Even the orchestra seemed trebled in size. Its members were dressed in the white powdered wigs and the knee-buckled livery of an eighteenth-century court orchestra. All in all, a striking sight—a throwback to what the audience must have seen at Esterhazy.

We all applauded the magnificence of the scene, as well as the man who'd brought it to us. Yera instead applauded the musicians as he walked down the stage steps and returned to his seat.

"They might have looked out through the curtain," he grumbled, but I noticed the tones turned to honey when he saw Hedda had slipped back beside him. Watch his hands, I radioed.

As the clapping died down, the musicians adjusted their music and turned to the concertmaster for his downbow signal. Rather ambitious it was, tackling this work without a conductor. But the opening Allegro Assai was played with such grace and elan that I listened closely, absorbed by their performance.

During the calmer Adagio, I glanced upward to see how Thorne was reacting. He had already surrendered to sleep, so I concluded his review would concentrate on the first movement. They often do.

While the third movement progressed, there was much commotion in one of the boxes above me. Somebody returning to his seat and making heavy weather of it. Only a blind man could knock over that many chairs.

The musicians then plunged into the Finale. It is during the Adagio of this last movement that, two by two, they pack up and leave. First, a horn and an oboe player snuff their candles and steal away. The music continues with two musicians missing from this game of musical chairs. Then another horn and oboe quash their candles and disappear. Then the contrabass, the cello, and the third and fourth violins gradually abandon the stage, while the musical forces grow ever more diminished. The viola, too, descends into outer darkness, until only the first and second violins remain. Then they, too, utter their final passage—the dismal notes of a descending minor chord—quench the last flames of light, and leave.

So it was here. For timeless seconds that seemed an eternity, no one spoke or moved. We were in that frame of silence.

Suddenly—in the still darkness—shots rang out.

Have you ever noticed that panic always follows gunfire? Every time, count on it.

In the Hall of Mirrors, panic was widespread.

"Let's get out of here!"

"I can't see!"

"The doors. Find the doors!"

"Turn on the lights, somebody!"

Well, who could blame them? Reverberating through the glass-lined hall, the sound still echoed from every space. No telling where it had come from.

There was commotion everywhere. The audience wanted to bolt but couldn't see where to bolt to.

"I think the shots were above us," I said to Yera. "You and Hedda stay here. I'll go upstairs."

Stumbling my way through assorted bodies, I pushed and shoved and edged my way toward the vestibule.

"Sorree, sir—or madam—you cannot go thees way." This from the security guard, still worried about burglaries and faithful to the last.

"Police!" I yelled. As good a ploy as any in the darkness. That made him move.

I plunged through the door into the pitch black of the vestibule. And I knew I was not alone in that narrow space. But whoever was in there with me was scurrying around like a rat finding his way out of a maze.

No exit.

Suddenly, the lights went on. I saw the broad back of a man dressed in black. He was fumbling at the patio door, which I could have told him was locked.

I took command of the situation as best I could.

"Citizen's arrest!" I cried.

As I may have mentioned earlier, I am not a big man. He was. Huge, bulky, and—with that gun in his hand—intimidating. I got a good look at that gun, since he turned toward me and aimed it right at my head. This seemed as good a time as any to leave.

As I backed out through the doorway, a shot pierced the air. Then another. And another.

Yera came rushing over.

"What happened! Are you all right!"

I checked my body for holes before replying.

"He's trapped—the gunman. The door's locked. I think he's shooting his way out."

Abruptly, the shooting stopped. So I peeked through the door. The heavy oak panel was hanging on its hinges. Nobody in there, though the acrid smell of gunpowder lay like a pall.

A police siren shattered the silence, then sounds of gunfire and shouted commands. From nowhere and from everywhere, security guards began crowding into the vestibule. Guns at the ready, now that all danger was past. Gingerly, they stepped out onto the terrace. This was hot pursuit? I could see a portion of the grounds, but the guns were exploding farther away.

Then I heard a woman's piercing scream above me. I rushed up the stairs.

The wail, unabated, came from the left side of the balcony. I followed it like a homing pigeon. The door to the first box was wide open. I rushed through the narrow anteroom to the jumble of chairs in front.

There stood Frieda Sweeten, the aged Medusa—tiara askew—still screaming. At her feet lay a body, a large and corpulent body.

I turned it over, sick with apprehension.

As I thought.

Sherrill Thorne would never write another bad review.

10

FRIEDA Sweeten went right on screaming, and I let her. The crowd would be here soon enough.

I knelt down on my knees and examined the mortal remains of Sherrill Thorne. Two bullets had passed through his body—one through the back of his head, the other through his back. There was not a sign of a heartbeat, so death must have come quickly for him. Without pain, I hoped.

His eyes were wide open—startled and bloodshot—his face red as always. There was an uncharacteristic disheveled look about him. One shirt sleeve had come undone; the other remained firmly anchored with his flat-sign cuff link. His collar, though still buttoned, was rumpled. I looked at him for some time. Then I placed my hands on his cold face to pull down the eyelids—

The police commissioner burst into the box just then.

"For God's sake, Frieda," said DaPonto to the hysterical woman, "shut up! What's the matter with you?"

She looked down at the prone body of Thorne and sank into the nearest chair. Her screams had ceased abruptly.

"I thought it was Vance," she said weakly. "But it's only that critic fellow. What a relief!" Then she got to her feet again. "I've got to get out of here and find my husband. He must be in the men's room. Again."

"Frieda, I've got to ask you some questions—"

"Anytime, Lorenzo. Right now, I've got to find Vance." So saying, she walked out on the spot.

And the police commissioner had to settle for me. "Was he like this when you found him?" he asked.

"No. He was lying on his face—"

"You had no right to move him, no right to touch a thing—"

"Yes, but—"

DaPonto cut short my excuses and briefly examined the body.

"Shot twice. Bullets went clean through him. The one in the back must have pierced his heart, but the one in the head alone would have killed him."

"Not a lot of blood."

"No, wouldn't be. Let's see—" He began checking the splintered wood below the balcony rail. "Here are the bullets. I'll have to have these photographed."

"Who is it?" said a voice close to us. We both looked up to see that the entire contingent of boxholders—more or less—had crowded onto the death scene.

"It's all right, folks," he said consolingly. "Nobody we know. It's only—what's his name again, Mr. Field?"

"Only the foremost music critic in the nation," I replied coldly. "His name is—was Sherrill Thorne."

"That's the fellow! We'll have this cleared up soon enough. My men are after his killer now. They'll round him up. Nothing for you to worry about! But I will have to ask you to leave the murder scene. Just a formality, you understand."

They left obediently, but I was reluctant to go. I tried to fade into the woodwork, but DaPonto noticed me there.

"You too, Mr. Field," he said. "I'll have to ask you to leave, too." He was on his knees again beside the body, but now he seemed more interested in Thorne's clothing than in Thorne's wounds. I watched as he emptied the contents of the critic's pockets onto his white linen handkerchief. Keys. Torn program. Kleenex. Nasal spray. A small plastic packet.

This last seemed to interest him. He held up the small packet by one of its corners and scrutinized the white powdery contents carefully.

"Out, I said, Mr. Field—"

"Could I see *your* credentials?" I said conversationally.

He turned to me in amazement. "My credentials?" he sputtered. "Why should you want to see my credentials? Everybody here knows who I am!"

"So they say. But aren't police officials required to carry identification at all times? I don't know who you are—beyond what others *say* you are."

"Christ! You're the stranger around here!"

"Exactly."

DaPonto seemed to be at that point where, were he a volcano, lava would have come spilling out at the seams. Now was the time to suggest a compromise, it seemed to me.

"Look," I said soothingly, "I know how hard it is to tuck much in the pockets of a tuxedo. So I'll take your word for it—about being police commissioner—if you'll let me stay. I may even be able to help you, you know."

"How?"

"I'm a murder buff myself, and I've had to—"

Like the comic strips where an electric light bulb appears above the head of the hero, DaPonto had caught on. "Oh, you're *that* John Field! I've heard plenty about you!"

From his tone, I had no inclination to ask what he had heard. And I was spared the trouble, anyway, by the appearance of a police officer in SWAT gear.

He saluted DaPonto briskly and reported, "We got him, sir!"

"Who?" asked DaPonto, not at all on top of it.

"The man fleeing the grounds. We shot him dead!" On his face was the euphoria that comes, I am told, from bagging a deer.

"Who called you?" I said. "How did you get here so fast?"

"I'll ask the questions, Mr. Field!" Then, turning to the officer, the commissioner said, "Who called you? How did you get here so fast?"

"Why, we've got a whole SWAT team patrolling the grounds. Part of the festival security precautions. Everybody thought you asked for it, sir!"

"Me? Me?" DaPonto collected himself and recollected. "Of course, it *had* to be me. With all the excitement, I'd just forgotten about it. I'd better go down and see the body. Do you want to go with me and see your friend's murderer, Mr. Field?"

"I'd like to see who shot Sherrill Thorne," I said.

It was a qualified answer.

* * *

The body lay on the ground near the heavy wrought-iron gates. Spotlights illuminated the grisly scene. I remembered a man dressed in black at the door, but no black was visible on this body. Only the red of burst arteries—the kind of damage caused when magnum bullets explode inside a man. Was that what they used down here? One way, I suppose, to fight crime. A brutal way, though.

DaPonto knelt down near the body and pointed to the arm outstretched above the dead man's head.

"See this?" he said. He pointed to a word—*Madre*—printed indelibly on the swarthy forearm. "He's a hit man. A Marielito hit man. I'll bet—" He turned the body over on its back and placed a finger inside the corpse's mouth. I looked at the still, heavy features, distorted by violent death. Same man I'd encountered at the Hall of Mirrors. But—

"I knew it!" said the police commissioner. He turned the dead man's lip inside out. I saw a number.

"That's the mark of a convict from one of Castro's prisons!" DaPonto stood up and brushed off his knees. "We'll have a file on him. That's how Cuba solved the problem of overcrowded jails. Sent them all over here. They all got involved with drug traffic as soon as they landed."

Two officers rushed up to the commissioner and drew him aside into whispered consultation. DaPonto looked pleased by their news. He handed them the little plastic bag from his handkerchief of evidence from Thorne's pockets and told them to "go to it—match it up."

"All over but the shooting," he said triumphantly to me, back at the body. An unfortunate turn of phrase. We were up to two corpses already, and the night was still young.

"While I appreciate your offer of help," he continued, "there's no need for it now. The case is all but solved. No mystery to it at all. Fits my hypothesis like a glove."

"Tell me about it."

"Sherrill Thorne obviously had a huge drug habit, which he hadn't the means to sustain. Or to pay for. So the drug mob used him as a courier."

"A what?"

"Courier—that means messenger."

"I understand a three-syllable word. What I don't understand is your theory."

"I neglected to tell you," said DaPonto smoothly. "The two officers you just saw were reporting on the search of Thorne's room. They found that Sherrill Thorne's suitcase was filled with kilos of cocaine."

"That's a lot of cocaine. Where were his pajamas?"

He ignored me and went on. "My belief is that the drug mob persuaded him to market the dope. Carry it up to New York City for them. After all, who would ever suspect the dean of American critics of carrying kilos of cocaine in his suitcase?"

"Only an idiot."

"And then perhaps he balked. Or he made outrageous demands. Or he wanted more money. Any number of scenarios come to mind."

"None of those."

"Why not? You yourself mentioned that Thorne never wanted to come to Fun City. He probably feared retribution."

"He feared the cultural scene. Who wouldn't? But Sherrill Thorne in drugs? Why, the whole idea is laughable!"

"You haven't had the experience in these matters that I've had, Mr. Field. You don't know what money does to people."

"Not to Thorne. He never got the chance. As for putting a foreign substance like cocaine into his body, why he would never—"

DaPonto cut me off shortly. "We may never know the whole truth," he said. "But I'm convinced that both killings were drug-related. And I'm relieved to see the whole mess cleared up so quickly. Swift justice. One on one. That's the way we do things down in Florida."

I didn't quite like the way they do things down in Florida. Maybe that was why I didn't mention to Lorenzo DaPonto that the Marielito who lay dead at the gates of Harmonia was no stranger to me.

Yes, he was the man I had found trying to escape the Hall of Mirrors, all right.

But more than that. He was the man I ran into at LaGuardia this morning.

The thug had almost knocked me down.

11

As we strode back through the grounds toward the mansion, I made a few guarded inquiries to DaPonto.

"When will you receive the autopsy report?" I asked.

"Autopsy? What autopsy? You can see the man was shot to death."

"That man, yes. I was speaking of Sherrill Thorne."

The commissioner looked at me in total astonishment. "What are you talking about?"

"I heard you tell the police officers to call the county coroner. I assume you're opening a full investigation into Thorne's death."

"Are you out of your mind? We have Thorne's murderer—"

"Are you sure?"

"Of course I'm sure. Do you really think you can walk into this town and tell me how to conduct a police investigation? Sure, I've called the coroner. Purely routine. He'll tell me what I already know—that Thorne is dead. For that, I don't need an autopsy. And I know who killed him. And for that, I don't need your help."

There seemed very little to say, after that. So we continued our walk in silence and reentered the Hall of Mirrors just as a bevy of police were escorting Thorne's body—wholly covered now by a sheet—through the silent crowd in the lobby.

Behind the stretcher hovered a portly, white-haired man whom I recognized from earlier in the evening as one of the more avid patrons of the bar. He had put down his drink long enough to pick up his black medical bag, so I suspected that he must be the coroner in question.

Right again. DaPonto greeted him jovially.

"Well, Frank," he said, "is he really dead?"

Frank looked blearily at the commissioner, then got him in focus.

"Couldn't be deader."

"How did he die?"

"Are you joking, Lorenzo?" The doctor hiccupped softly. "He was shot to death. Any fool knows that."

"Have you met Mr. Field?" I didn't like the timing after the medico's last sentence, but DaPonto went blithely on.

"Dr. Frank Closset—John Field. Mr. Field—Dr. Closset. You recognize Mr. Field, I'm sure, as our eminent pianist of the evening. Do you have the death certificate, by the way?"

"Naturally."

"Already?" I asked, somewhat shrilly.

"When you have seven hundred homicides a year, Mr. Field, you have to keep up with the paperwork." The coroner handed the document to the police commissioner, while dishing out praise to me. "Delighted to meet you in person. Wonderful Beethoven tonight."

I cast my eyes heavenward. Beethoven!

"Mr. Field is more than a pianist," added DaPonto. "He's something of a detective, too. He was just asking if I saw any need to order an autopsy on Sherrill Thorne's body."

Dr. Closset laughed heartily at the suggestion.

"Not unless you want to be up to your ears in bodies, Lorenzo. Not often we have it this easy, is it? Even an auditorium of eyewitnesses!"

Still chuckling mirthfully, the coroner wobbled off and left me with Fun City's finest. Wordlessly, Lorenzo DaPonto handed me the death certificate that Dr. Closset had given him. Bold as life, the coroner had written, "Cause of death: two gunshot wounds, one piercing the brain, one piercing the heart. Death instantaneous."

No complaint about confusing medical terminology there.

The doctor had signed his name to the certificate in a large, sprawling script that trailed off the page.

Without a word, I handed the document back to the police commissioner. We both knew that the death certificate—signed, sealed, and delivered—marked the end of the official police investigation.

And I knew that my own investigation must begin now. Before the murderer struck again.

"I wonder," said I to DaPonto, "what other damage that Marielito did around here."

He let my remark die on the tropical air.

The crowd had thinned out in the marble lobby, now that the evening seemed to offer no more surprises.

No attempt had been made to detain anyone. The audience, as a result, was making a quick getaway. I watched as scores of people climbed into assorted Rolls-Royces, Mercedes-Benzes, Cadillacs, and Chryslers and departed the grounds of Harmonia with speed that surprised me. I marveled as the local musicians—the Haydn orchestra—piled into one Volkswagen van and departed at full throttle. It was going to be one full ferry back to the mainland.

In no time at all, we were down to our band of musicians—all of us staying here at Harmonia—and to the permanent residents of Key Cohen. Looking around, I realized that these residents (the entire audience residue) were none other than the boxholders, the members of the festival board, the really *special* givers that Eric Hanson had described. Interesting.

All alone near a portico, the beauteous Hedda Hasse stood forlornly, abandoned—it would seem—by her aged suitor. So I moved in fast.

"Where's Mr. Yera?" I asked, by way of pretext.

"In bed, I think. Tonight's events were a great shock to him. And he's not well, you know."

"I saw him briefly in Thorne's box after the murder. He looked badly shaken."

"More than you know. He thinks those bullets were intended for him."

It was my turn to be shaken. "What do you mean?" I asked.

"Didn't you know? Mr. Yera arranged for Thorne to have

his box just a few minutes before the concert began. Tony always sits there because the acoustics in the hall are excellent at that point.''

I didn't know which information confused me more—the seat switch and its implications, or the contradictory forms of address used by the singer in referring to the composer. I tried to concentrate on the seat switch.

"Surely Yera can't think that Sherrill Thorne looked anything like him."

"They were both bald."

"But Thorne was fat, and Yera is thin. Thorne was tall and Yera is—"

"—of medium height."

"I can't believe," I said, "that any hit man worth his salt would mistake his victim. Thorne wasn't killed by accident."

"Was Sherrill Thorne a good friend of yours?"

"Why do you ask?"

"Because you seem to be taking this personally. I thought perhaps you had built up a friendship over the years. I mean— well, it's a brutal way to die, and I can understand how you must feel. Even if what they're saying is true."

"That ridiculous hypothesis about drugs?"

"That must be very difficult for you to accept."

I thought about that before I answered. Sherrill Thorne had inhabited the same small musical world as I, though on opposite sides of the fence. We were not friends. He was a professional listener, and I was a professional performer. Often, he had hurt me—as he hurt many others—with a review that took a cheap shot or that simply placed me in a niche.

But there were times—rare times, I'll admit—when I sensed he was motivated by the same intense love of music as I. No one asks for that. It's a deformity that cripples and isolates you from what all the rest of the world holds dear.

And those of us who yield to that love can seldom expect much material reward. (Always excepting, of course, conductors and opera singers.) Even if we're exceptionally skilled in our craft. As I am. As Thorne, I had to grudgingly admit, was. Now that he was gone, I knew I'd miss him. All things considered, he was a worthy adversary.

And a drug peddler as well? Hedda had posed that very

question. Before answering, I took her by the arm and steered her back into the brightly lit Hall of Mirrors.

"Thorne into drug dealing? That's impossible for me to accept," I said. "He would never do anything so sordid. Besides, this was the second attempt on Thorne's life, and this attempt succeeded."

"How did I miss the first one?" she asked.

"You didn't. You sat through it all." A creature of habit, I guided the singer to the front row we had occupied earlier. "That was not your run-of-the-mill forced landing this morning. The plane was sabotaged."

"How? By who?"

"Whom," I corrected her. "You remember that I was the last one to board the plane this morning?"

"Yes. It was an entrance to remember."

"Well, on my way, I almost collided with a mechanic coming back from the plane. From underneath, near the oil tanks."

"So?"

"He was rushing from and I was rushing to that plane. We bumped into each other, and I saw him very clearly."

"I don't see—"

"I saw him here again tonight. He was the man I found shooting his way out through the door."

"The one the police shot?"

"The one everybody shot," I said. "The Marielito."

She seemed relieved. An odd reaction.

"How can you be sure it was the same man? You must have seen him very briefly."

"I have a good memory for faces. Besides, I noticed a tattoo on his arm when he waved me toward the plane. The corpse outside had the same tattoo."

"You are observant."

I basked. Why argue with truth?

"But why do you—" she began.

"Yes?" I allowed the question.

"Even though the plane was sabotaged—probably by a slow oil leak—why—"

"Would he show up here tonight?" I anticipated the question. "To finish the job, naturally. Our forced landing was telecast all over the country. It's the news of the moment—

up to now. Once the Marielito knew his first attempt failed, he had to come down and—''

''Oh, I understand all that.'' She dismissed my lucid explanation with a wave of the hand. ''But why do you think the man's presence there—or his death here—eliminates the possibility that Thorne was involved in drug dealing?''

I looked at her impatiently. ''Well, I knew Thorne and you didn't. He simply wasn't the type.''

''I hear everybody's the type. Doctors, lawyers, students—''

''He had no *reason*. He was old and lonely but, in his way, content. The only one who meant anything in the world to him—his wife—died some years ago. And he's adjusted as well as could be expected to her death.''

''Maybe she was ill a long time. Maybe he had such huge medical bills to pay, he had to turn to drug peddling—''

''Not Sherrill Thorne. They frown on that sort of thing at the *Globe*. That job meant more to him than any amount of money.''

''My understanding is that he was all but out of a job at the *Globe*. They give him an assignment now and then as a kind of sop. I heard the paper was furious with him for reviewing a concert that he didn't know had been canceled.''

''A canard, my dear. That story is told about every critic who ever folded up his tent and walked away. Some secondrate stringer who wanted Thorne's job propounded that lie.''

Ms. Hasse looked appropriately contrite. She did deliver one parting salvo, though in the sweetest possible tones.

''I don't know what you're suggesting. No one knew Thorne here. If you reject the only possible explanation—that Thorne was involved with drugs and the drug ring had him gunned down—what else is left? Do you know something I don't?''

I hedged. ''Well, it's out of character, that's all. Thorne never acted out of character. And the man had integrity.''

''A few hours ago, I don't think you'd have given such a testimonial to Thorne's character. I read his last review of you.''

Intelligence, now and then, rears its ugly head among singers. Not often does it do so, though, in a young woman of

Ms. Hasse's measurements. I say this with no trace of chauvinism. Simply wonder.

Wonder is the only explanation for my revealing to Hedda Hasse what I fully intended to keep to myself. For the time being, anyway. I heaved a mighty sigh and told all.

"All right, then. But don't breathe a word of this. I don't think our supposed assassin killed Thorne at all."

"But you heard the shots! You saw a man with a gun in his hands seconds later! The coroner has certified that Thorne died of gunshot wounds. And surely the caliber of the bullets in Thorne's body can be checked against the bullets in the hit man's gun."

I paused before answering and looked around at our surroundings in the blinding artificial light.

"I don't care what the doctor has certified. Or why. Remember, I was the first person to examine Thorne's body."

"Were you? I didn't know that."

"Well, I was. The first thing I noticed was that the body was stone cold. It should still have been warm—within minutes after a shooting. More than that—the bullets struck both the head and the chest. Yet there was virtually no blood at all, where there should have been a tremendous pool of blood."

"That's odd," she agreed. "Even though Thorne was clinically dead, doesn't it take more than a few seconds for all bodily functions to cease?"

"Usually—especially with shooting deaths. But by the time I got to Thorne—within five minutes of the shooting—he was stone-cold dead. And there is no other explanation for that, but that he was dead before the assassin shot him. Long before."

Miss Ice-Eyes looked at me in total astonishment. She really had remarkable eyes—laser beams, they were. Good for scrutinizing faces for hidden truths. Very hard to lie to those eyes.

"You realize," she said slowly, "that if you're right, that opens up a whole new field of possibilities."

"And suspects, too."

"It would mean that the Marielito was himself—"

"Set up. Did that never occur to you?"

"No—not at all." She pondered awhile. "But you said that

the coldness of Thorne's body was the first thing you noticed. Did you notice something else, too?''

I hesitated. "I can't be sure," I began, forgetting that my listener was a singer with a keen ear for vocal nuances.

"You mean," she flared, "you can't be sure about me!"

In a fury, she got up and left. Since she had the broken foot—not me—I headed her off at the pass and sat her down again at an aisle seat.

"Look, you've got a bad case of divided loyalties. I don't know what camp you're in—Fun City's or the music world's. And believe me, the two are incompatible."

"Like us!" She scrambled to her feet once more, forcing me to take her firmly by the shoulders and push her back into the seat.

"You remind me," I said, "of the prima donna who told her audience that she liked to keep one foot in Boston and one foot in Philadelphia."

"So?"

"Until a voice from the crowd shouted out, 'Look out, New York!' "

"That's vile."

"Only if you're in New York."

Temperament came easily to this child, though she surprised me now. She began to laugh, and she laughed until the tears rolled down her cheeks. Then she started to cry uncontrollably. Nerves, I guess. The shocks of the day. She looked so young and vulnerable to me at that moment.

Unaccountably, I found her hand in mine, and I heard myself muttering words that I never—not in a million years—planned to say aloud.

"What do I know about you?" I asked. "Except that I'm enormously attracted to you—who wouldn't be?—and that you have the makings of an artist."

"Hell," she sniffed through her tears, "isn't that enough? What do I know about you, either?"

She had a point. Rather, the first question was valid; the second bordered on libel.

"At the very least," I said, somewhat stiffly, "you know I have some reputation as a—"

"Pianist—well, naturally, I know *that*."

"—truth sleuth, I was going to say. And there's no question about whose side I'm on. I'm always on the side of the angels.' "

"And you think I'm not? You think I'm as blasé as everyone else in this town at the sight of violent death?"

"I hope not. On the other hand, I can't see any reason why you'd want to help me. But I hope you will."

"What can I tell you?"

"You know the people here. You know what motivates them, and you know something of their backgrounds. Besides that, you're familiar with Harmonia, the scene of the crime."

"Yes, I can help you there. You know what the natives call Harmonia, don't you? They call it 'The House That Jack Built.' "

I looked puzzled.

"Jack—in the sense of money. It's probably the most costly mansion ever built in Florida. Maybe that's what makes it such a source of fascination for the people here."

"I'm convinced that the solution to this crime lies here, somehow. And I tend to focus in on a very small group of people—the ones who paid $300,000 or more for the privilege of sitting near Sherrill Thorne. Do you realize that the people sitting in the balcony were the only ones who had free access to Thorne's box? You were up there. Can you tell me who was the last person to leave him there? The last one to see him alive?"

She took such a long time answering that I thought she hadn't heard me.

But finally she spoke.

"I think it was me," she said at last. "No—I'm *positive* it was me."

12

I was stunned into silence.

"What are you trying to say?" I asked.

"You asked who was the last person in Thorne's box. I said it was me."

"There's your error," I said. "You should have said 'It was I.' A predicate nominative must be interchangeable in number and case with the subject noun or pronoun. It is a violation of English grammar to use the pronoun *me* as a predicate nominative, because that incorrectly substitutes a direct object."

Hedda Hasse looked at me in some surprise.

I excused her. "It's a common mistake," I said.

"Getting on with the murder," she said with a trace of asperity, "why did you ask who was the last person in Sherrill Thorne's box?"

With anybody else, I would have replied candidly, "Because suspicion logically falls on the last person to see the murder victim alive." And I could have added, "Without exception, the last person to see the murder victim alive is the murderer."

I did not explain any of this to Ms. Hasse because of her implied rebuff of my elucidation of the proper use of the predicate nominative. I mean—the last thing I want to be accused of is being a bore.

As Fate had it, an interruption spared me further pursuit of this line of questioning. We'd been chatting in the bright lights of the auditorium, both of us seated just a few rows up from the seats where we had watched the Haydn performance.

Just then, a security guard came walking down the aisle and informed us—in heavily accented English—that he would be locking up in a few minutes. I recognized him as the guard who had delayed me in my pursuit of the armed intruder. The one, you'll recall, who wouldn't let me through the vestibule door after the shots were fired.

"Just a minute, please," I said to him. "I'd like to inspect this hall before you close it."

Uncomprehending, the guard looked at me and then at Hedda, who provided a rapid Spanish translation.

"Jokay, Miss Jedda." He smiled disarmingly and turned to leave, but I wasn't finished yet.

"Hedda, ask him where the security guards were stationed tonight. Where, and how many, and how assigned."

"You mean—all night? During the entire performance?"

"Yes. It's important."

She launched into a tirade of Spanish that, to my untutored ear, sounded like a small, cross terrier yipping in the night. He replied volubly and even faster. She interrupted frequently with questions, so that eventually the dialogue resembled nothing so closely as two schnauzers fighting fiercely.

How the ear can deceive! The guard retreated from the hall, wreathed in smiles, on the carpet of *graciases* from my companion.

"Well?" I asked.

"He says he was in charge of all the security guards—his name is Luis Rodriguez, by the way—and he gave them their instructions. So he knows where they all were or where they should have been. He guarded the door at the left side of the hall, that's the sole access to the balcony area from the auditorium. He let in only three people through that door all evening—Antonio Yera and myself, during intermission, and you, after the shots were fired. Even after that, he wouldn't allow anyone other than the guards and the police through that door."

"I remember. Conscientious to a fault."

"There was a guard on the private terrace," continued Hedda, "both before the performance and during intermission. He locked the entrance door both times, after the balcony boxholders were all inside. Luis questioned him, and the guard said he knew all the boxholders."

"Lucky there wasn't a fire," I commented. "Everybody in the balcony would have been trapped inside."

"I thought of that, too. If the gunman was trapped inside, so was everybody in the balcony. But the guard reminded me that the deadbolt lock was never used during performances—just the simple latch lock on the doorknob. The boxholders could go outside—but no one could come in from outside."

"Yet someone did."

Hedda mulled this over and replied. "He could have gotten into the hall long before the performance and waited for his moment."

"That's possible," I agreed reluctantly. "But why would he wait so long? Why wait until the performance was over? Where was the rest of the security guard contingent?"

"Two stood inside the auditorium at the rear doors. There was no guard at the right vestibule. That has an open archway leading to the downstairs lounges.

"And three guards," she went on, "guarded the lobby entrance from the courtyard outside. One of these guards was temporarily posted in the private terrace—but I've already told you about him."

"So," I summarized, "half the security team guarded the interior of the Hall of Mirrors during the entire performance—two at the rear doors and one at the left door leading to the vestibule. And the other half stood outside, with one guard posted to the terrace for two short periods. No guards in the balcony area?"

"No. None at all. Luis said that was why it was so important that he watch the vestibule door and why he had to check everyone going in and out. The boxholders objected to seeing so many armed guards around. It made them nervous, he said."

"Nervous as they were, they left the stage doors unguarded. I wonder why. Do you suppose they trust musicians? Let's go check the wings."

Our remarks filled the silence of the empty hall as we ascended the open stage steps and passed into the wings.

"Do you expect to find something?" asked Hedda. "Surely the police have already searched every inch of the Hall of Mirrors."

"No, they haven't. They don't intend to." And I told her, briefly, of my conversation with Lorenzo DaPonto and the hasty closing of the case before any investigation had even begun.

"You mustn't be too hard on him," she said. "Key Cohen is so wealthy, it can afford its own police department. The citizens who appointed him are the patrons of this festival."

"He's not even an elected official? He's not even answerable to the voters of Fun City?"

"Oh, they have their *own* police commissioner. Key Cohen is completely independent of Fun City—even though it's surrounded on three sides by it. So you can imagine how powerful are the citizens who own the estates on this key."

"The police commissioner owes his job to them. That's what you're saying."

"Yes, but I don't think he'd scuttle a murder investigation."

"He just did," I pointed out. "Do you know DaPonto well?"

"I don't know anybody well here—I know a few people who have introduced me to a few more people—and all those contacts have helped me get started."

"In singing—or in real estate?"

"Both," she said. "The two interests are not mutually incompatible."

"They are—like night and day. But we'll talk about that later."

I noticed a small cabinet to the right of the stage door. It lay at about chin level. My chin, of course.

"Do you suppose this could be the fusebox?" I asked. I opened the hinged door and found that was exactly what it was.

"Anybody," said Hedda, "could have slipped out in the darkness and pulled that master switch."

"Perhaps," I agreed, "but this cabinet blends so closely

with the paint of the wall that it would be almost impossible to see it—unless you knew what you were looking for.''

I closed the fusebox cabinet and stepped toward the door to the vestibule, before I recalled that the gunman had been trapped out there, unable to escape through this stage door.

"This will still be locked," I said.

"It's never locked. We all went in that way."

"*We* went in that way. The other musicians came in through the opposite wings. Don't you remember they were all milling about when we came off the stage?"

"Here—it must be stuck." She fiddled about with the doorknob until the door did swing open.

I led the way into the small vestibule. It was like going back to sleep and resuming the same nightmare. To our right, the door leading out to the terrace swung eerily on its hinges. The brass doorknob and lock had been blasted from their moorings, but a few strands of molten brass clung to the door like survivors on a life raft.

For a few seconds, we gazed in silence. Then Hedda shuddered—a rippling movement of those exquisite, square shoulders.

"Someone walking on your grave?" I asked. "Do you want to leave? There's no reason for you to stay if you don't want to."

"No—no—I want to. Let me show you the boxes, then we'll leave."

She led the way up the curved marble staircase, as agile as a fawn. A slightly wounded fawn, to be sure. I noted, with great approval, her lithe grace and proud carriage. A little work with her bows—that was all that was needed—and she would reduce audiences to helpless, hand-clapping adoration.

"Why is this the only entry to the boxes?" I asked.

"For ultraprivacy, I guess. That's the way Joseph Lange redesigned it. It may even have been an architectural error. Everyone complains that there's no access to the lobby from the boxes. And vice versa."

The steps fanned out at the top and opened to a U-shaped hallway. To our left, at the end of the hallway, a magnificent arched window stretched from floor to ceiling, its red draperies accenting the color of the hall's thick carpeting. I walked straight to the window and pulled aside the folds of draperies.

"Do you smell that acrid odor?" I asked.

"It must be from the vestibule. The smell of gunpowder."

"No. It's right here."

A few minutes' investigation, and I found the cause. A cigarette had been ground into the carpeting. As good a way as any to put out a cigarette, I suppose, but hard on the carpeting. I remembered that there were no ashtrays in Harmonia.

"A sneak smoker among the balcony patrons?" suggested Hedda.

"Hardly. They had their private terrace for smoking. No, someone was hiding here—long enough to smoke a Camel."

"That would take a real man. Do you think it was the Marielito?"

"Makes sense," said I laconically.

We opened the door of the nearest box. Thorne's box. A chalk mark outlined the spot where the critic's body had lain. A deep scar on the balcony wall gave silent testimony to the bullets that had ripped through Sherrill Thorne and lodged into the wood railing. But the bullets had already been removed.

I saw no more indications of the tragedy that had occurred here tonight, aside from some scraps from Thorne's program. DaPonto, I recalled, had placed the remaining portion in his handkerchief.

"It's too late to find anything new here now. I just want to see things from here. Thorne always sat alone, you know. Insisted on it. Can you remember who sat where in the rest of the boxes?"

Hedda frowned (a beguiling frown) and tried to visualize the scene.

"I only looked up here when we came out on the stage. I'm not sure I can remember where everyone was."

"Try, anyway. Together, we may piece it together."

"I noticed that Rachael Radler was in the center box. She always gets the best seat, since she's our local impresario."

"I know her—she announced the football scores, too. Wasn't she with someone?"

"Her husband Richard. He's easy to forget. He walks in her shadow at all times."

"Her shadow is hard to avoid. But weren't there others in this box?"

"The Argentos. He's the old diplomat, and she's the young Latin beauty. You remember her from the receiving line?"

"Indeed I do. Are there only seven boxes in the balcony?"

"That's right—three on each side and one in the center. That was all there was room for in this small theater. Perhaps Antonio Yera decided on that number because of his interest in numerology. There are seven letters in his first name. He's a great one for buried clues, you know."

No, I didn't know, but I remembered how Sherrill Thorne had harped away on that point.

"Did he build the entire mansion, do you know? It has the look of a building dating from the seventeenth century."

"Nothing dates from the seventeenth century here. The stones were imported, slab by slab, from a French château to *look* like it dates from a long time ago."

"Who sat in the box next to Thorne's?"

Hedda screwed up her eyes to think. "The Sweetens, I believe. The old general and his wife."

"Frieda Sweeten lodged herself in my mind right off," I said. "She found the body."

"Well, she was closest. The general couldn't have found the body if he fell over it. He has severe cataracts."

"Can he hear? Or why does he come to concerts?"

"He hears everything. All his other senses—hearing, smell, taste, and touch—are excellent. Often the case with blind— or near-blind—people. You'll find him, by the way, the most informed music lover down here. Let me see," she continued, "I do remember seeing Joseph Lange on the left. That's the artist, you know, with the big head and all the hair. I noticed him when I came onstage."

"Over there?" I pointed opposite to the second box on the right balcony.

"No, that's where the arts chairman sat—Connie Weber and her dear friend Miguel. Joseph Lange was one box farther down. I didn't notice who was with him—probably Bob O'Reilly, the lawyer you met at the reception. He and Lange are great friends."

"Where was Antonio Yera sitting?"

"Directly opposite this box. It's the closest counterpart to this one in acoustics and sightlines."

"Well, that accounts for every box but one. Who are we forgetting?"

"Whom," she corrected, getting even for the predicate nominative. "I know—the police commissioner and his wife. The DaPontos sat two boxes up from Sherrill Thorne."

"I wonder why it took him so long to reach Thorne's box?"

"Maybe he ran the wrong way," Hedda suggested. "It was hard to tell what direction the shots came from."

"His wife was the vision in pink. Does she always dress like a fairy godmother?"

"No, sometimes she comes as a vampire. I really feel sorry for her. I guess being married to Lorenzo would force anybody into a fantasy world."

We left Thorne's box and silently inspected the remaining boxes. Though mirrors lined the walls there too, their effect was softened by the full draperies that enclosed and enshrouded each module. I checked the sightlines to the stage: each box had a clear view of the platform and of the box directly opposite, but a limited view of the adjoining boxes.

"Is there anything else we should see up here?"

"There are lounges to the right—directly above the lounges downstairs."

"But these are restricted to balcony patrons?"

"Yes. Another privilege for the biggest donors to the arts center. That's why I happened to come up here during intermission—there was such a line downstairs. I bumped into Lisa and Connie there, and they insisted on taking me over and introducing me to Sherrill Thorne."

"I'm surprised he didn't bite your heads off. It looked like a pilgrimage to the Holy Land from where I sat."

"Well, Rachael Radler told me that the fact that a New York critic was coming down to review the dedicatory performance simply *made* the festival. Unbelievable, she said, what that did for fund-raising."

We had reached the right portion of the U-shaped hallway, and Hedda pointed the way toward the lounges. I learned that men's rooms are the same the world over, but that this ladies' room had to set a new standard for sumptuousness. (Not that

I could be *sure,* naturally.) Then I emerged, and we began retracing our steps to the staircase.

The door to one of the boxes had been left open. As I went to close it, I noticed a quick reflection—the back of some-one's head, repeated to infinity in the angled mirrors.

Then nothing.

Firmly, I grasped Hedda Hasse by the arm and said, "We'll check the rest of the hall later."

"Don't you want to see—"

"It can wait—"

I rushed her right along. But not nearly fast enough.

The lights—all of them—went out again in the Hall of Mirrors.

With a brusqueness alien to my nature, I pushed the singer into the closest balcony box, where we crawled on all fours toward the farthest corner and crouched beneath two chairs.

No sound at all.

"Maybe it's a power failure," whispered Hedda.

"Likely story."

"Maybe I should scream for help."

"And reveal our location?"

I must have managed to do that, for we heard the quick patter of footsteps across the marble floor of the auditorium below. The sound was coming toward us.

"I think he found the fusebox," my companion murmured. "Do you think he's coming up here?"

"Somebody is."

We heard the clatter of heavy shoes against the staircase, then the abrupt cessation of all sound as the intruder reached the top of the stairs and proceeded quietly along the thickly carpeted hallway.

The creak of a door and the swift, searching beam of a flashlight placed the pursuer. He (She? It?) was in Thorne's box, almost directly opposite us. I waited for the light to disappear, then I peered out over the balcony rail.

"It's not much of a drop from here to the auditorium," I said softly. "No more than fifteen feet. Do you think you can make it?"

No reply. I had forgotten about her foot.

"I'm sorry. Stupid of me."

"You jump," she whispered. "I'll be all right here. You *know* you can get out through the vestibule door to the terrace. That door's been blown off."

"Quiet!"

We watched and waited as the flashlight illuminated the contents of the box bordering Thorne's. The searcher was thorough. We could hear him overturning chairs. Finally, the light disappeared again.

In a choked voice, I hissed, "Think of something else! I'm not going to run for help while you get shot."

"You think of something! You're the detective!"

The light appeared. And disappeared. Closer now.

"We don't have too many choices," I pointed out, sotto voce. "We jump, or we run for it. Or we stay here like sitting ducks."

Another door opened. Now the beam searched the box right next to us. Here the light lingered a long, long time, its shining mirrored incessantly throughout the Hall. Fireflies in a moonless night. Then blackness.

"Stand behind the door," I said. "It opens in. He won't see you at first. I'll trip him before he does."

This said with confidence masking despair, Hedda scooted to the assigned spot. I picked up a chair in the darkness and stood to the opposite side of the door. Not an easy task. The chair was heavy—a dead weight.

The door opened slowly. The light shone on Hedda and me. We could see ourselves mirrored very clearly.

That's all we could see. I crashed the chair down with all my might.

And missed.

"Meester Feeld," said a soft Latin voice. "You cannot move anytheeng around in here. Deedn't I tell you that?"

13

WE should have guessed, of course.

It was the chief security guard—Luis Rodriguez.

Helpful as always. Doing his job. Checking the hall.

I picked up the overturned chair quickly, apologetically, with some fatuous comment about wanting "to see how it looked over here." My crashing blow had made only a slight thump on the carpet. Could have been anything.

"Really, Luis," said Hedda from her post behind the door. "Why didn't you say something?"

He flashed the torch on her. Then on me. Then he put two and two together and naturally reached sex.

"Sorree to deesturb you, Mees Jedda. Pleez—go on weeth—weeth whatever you were doeeng."

"See here—" I began, in the iciest tone possible.

"Don't be silly, Luis," snapped Hedda. "Give us those keys, and we'll finish locking up for you. Is that the complete set?"

The security guard scratched his head and looked down at the stout keyring in his hand.

"I canna understand eet. The deadbolt key was meesing—for the door to the terrace—but now eet ees here. And the key to the box—where the man was shot—that was meesing, too."

"Is it there now?" I asked.

"No—ees still gone."

"Have you mentioned this to anyone?"

"Yes—I tell Meester Yera. Then I tell him I found the deadbolt key. He says the box key ees probably someplace on the ring, too, and that I have too many keys on eet. But ees not here."

"Does anybody else have access to these keys?"

Luis looked to Hedda Hasse for clarification, and she supplied a quick translation of his reply.

"He says no. He could have set them down for a few minutes in the excitement tonight, but he can't recall doing so. Normally, he carries the keyring with him. And he says he's put a heavy chain on the door that was blown off, so we can't go in or out that way."

"That's a relief—neither can anyone else." As an afterthought, I added, "Did he lend that keyring to anybody at any time?"

The dialogue between Hedda and the guard began in earnest this time, with frequent excited yelps from the security guard.

"He says absolutely not," reported Hedda finally. "That would be a betrayal of trust. During the festival preparations, though, Mr. Yera told him to lend the keys to any of the board members who asked for them."

"Such as—"

"General and Mrs. Vance Sweeten, Joseph Lange, Rachael and Richard Radler—"

"Everyone in the balcony, in short?"

"Every last one."

We finished off what little inspection remained, but our hearts weren't in it anymore. Then I escorted Hedda back to her room in the tower opposite mine. She did not invite me in. Not that I—well, never mind.

I trudged back across the courtyard and took the elevator up to my own room. But was bedtime in the cards even now? Not a chance.

There sat the violinist James Goldman in the large armchair in my room. All set to pounce on me.

"Thanks to you," he began straight off, "I suppose we're all suspects for murder. Isn't that right? There isn't a one of us who wouldn't have cheerfully murdered Thorne, given half a chance and a clear escape."

Goldman was in no mood to be coherent. He launched into a classic harangue, a temper tantrum so outraged and self-indulgent that I simply stopped listening. I knew what was bothering him. He was experiencing a case of post-concert nerves, that inevitable letdown that follows every performance. The murder that followed tonight's performance virtually erased all memory of the night's achievement. And he realized that.

"A performance unique in the annals of music," wailed Goldman, "and Thorne gets himself murdered to upstage us!"

"Not intentionally, I'm sure."

"He'd do it! He'd do it! He never liked me, you know."

"You're wrong. He admired you greatly."

"As an artist. But as a person, he never liked me at all. It would please him to think that I—along with everybody else—was under suspicion in his death."

"That's ridiculous. Where did you hear that?"

Goldman didn't bother to answer my question. "I'm not staying, you know," he said. "It was a mistake to come down here in the first place, and I absolutely *am not staying!* I'm running out of fiddle strings—you can be sure there's no place around here to replenish my supply—and I'm playing in Mexico City on Monday, and I absolutely will not cancel that engagement!"

"You won't have to," I said wearily. "The police think they've solved this case. None of us are suspects."

Goldy stopped short.

"Why not?" he asked. "Any one of us could have fired those shots. And most of us had good reason. The darkness took away everybody's alibi. Gave all of us an opportunity."

I sat on my bed and untied my shoes. This was a gentle hint to Goldman that his host was sick of being hospitable.

"They shot the man they think fired the shots at Thorne. The police think they've got their man."

"If they shot him dead, how can they be sure?"

"My point exactly."

I placed all the contents from my pockets on the lamp table

beside me, vaguely conscious that the contents didn't look the same as they had earlier in the evening.

"I'm as anxious as the next man to get out of here," sputtered Goldy, "but I can't see letting somebody get by with murder simply because it's too much trouble to find out the truth."

"I thought you wanted to get out of here."

"Surely you know me better than to take me seriously when I'm upset. Naturally, I want to get out of here, but—"

"Well, nobody will stop you. They're only too happy to place this on the head of the man they shot."

"Now, tell me honestly, John. Do *you* think that was the murderer?"

I was examining the objects on the table—a crushed handkerchief, a torn ticket stub, a cuff link, a nail clipper.

"Well?" prompted Goldy.

"Oh, no. It was impossible that he was the murderer. Absolutely impossible."

"Now I didn't say we had to entirely rule him out. I just want to be fair and consider all the possibilities."

"Well, you can forget about that one."

"Why?"

Befogged bewilderment is not an expression you're liable to see on the distinguished countenance of James Goldman most days of the week. But it was there now.

I put on my pajamas and robe and rose to indicate that the evening's conversation was over.

"You mentioned something," I said, "about violin strings and the lack of them. Tell me, were you missing a violin string after the performance?"

"Yes. A D string was gone. How on earth did you know that?"

"You implied it earlier. And I knew it had to be something like that. Strong. Easy to filch. Yes, a violin string would be perfect—"

"What are you talking about?"

"And so accessible. Every violinist in the world carries extra strings around."

I had led the way to the door, and now I opened it to push the violinist through if need be.

"What does it matter that one of my fiddle strings was

missing? What has that got to do with anything? Sherrill
Thorne was shot, wasn't he?''

Closing the door firmly, I said, ''No, Goldy, he was strangled. Furthermore, he'd been strangled much earlier in the
evening. Our gunman shot a corpse.''

Goldy gave a short but sincere yelp of pain.

I had forgotten his foot was in the door.

To my shame, I slept like a babe. And awoke next morning
hungry as a hungry bear. Full of vim and vip and hackneyed
expressions, which I attributed to the salt air. More likely,
Thorne's sad fate had made me glad, on this beautiful morning, to be alive.

The common reaction, I think, for I found all the musicians at breakfast on the long flagstone patio facing Bilboa
Bay. They were contentedly helping themselves to the offer-
ings of an enormous buffet table and were carting back their
plates to small, graceful iron tables etched with the inevitable
sharp signs.

White-coated waiters hovered about with bottles of champagne. A chef de cuisine smilingly dispensed slabs of beef,
ham, and pork, while we helped ourselves to mountains of
shrimp, scrambled eggs, and pancakes.

There was no black coffee. I settled for a thimble-size cup
of mucous brown substance said to be Cuban coffee (an eye-
opener, let me tell you) when I saw Seamus Connacht waving
at me to join his table.

Seamus is a shameless blatherskite who has hung by his
heels, as the saying goes. He is also a lucid, charming rascal
who knows the soothing power of words. Today, he was giving us a virtuoso performance.

''We won't talk about anythin' 'til we eat,'' he said. And
we didn't. He did. He asked me if it was true that Debussy
turned to a companion in the middle of a Beethoven symphony and said, ''Let's go—he's starting to develop.''

He had a wealth of stories about opera stars, all too scur-
rilous to be quoted here.

We ate and we listened and we laughed, citing episodes
from the past when we were all starting out in this hazardous
profession, where talent counts but chutzpah helps. Finally,
even the silver-tongued Connacht ran out of words. We all

sat in silence and stared at the breathtaking seascape before us.

Blue-green sea merged with sun and clouds and heavens. Sailboats bobbed up and down on the still water like toys in a gigantic bathtub. A pelican—that ungainly but efficient bird—swooped down on the water, scooped up a small fish, and returned to shore for a leisurely meal. In the tropical foliage that bordered the bay, a white heron lifted one delicate foot and surveyed us Homo sapiens with great disdain.

So—then and there—Seamus Connacht posed the question that had been plaguing us all.

"How do you suppose Antonio Saul Yera stands it down here?"

Everyone joined the chorus.

"Not even a symphony orchestra."

"Nor a decent museum."

"Or a first-class university or a conservatory or an arts school."

"Or a theater, either."

"What do they do with themselves here?" asked Ted Holzman. "Does everybody grow up to be a football player or a football fan?"

"Let's be fair," I said. "You're discounting such cultural phenomena as the Porpoise Palace."

"What happens there?" asked a wide-eyed Connacht.

"I am told that a corps of dolphins swims in the water while beautiful maidens ride on their backs. Then the maidens get off, and the dolphins rise out of the water and pirouette in time to rock music. For an encore, a killer whale comes out, swims around, turns over, and splashes water on everybody. This, as you may guess, is the highlight of the afternoon."

"Sounds really great," said Connacht, in tones of wonder. "I wouldn't want to miss that. All this—and Mickey Mouse not a day away."

"We must also take note," I went on, "of Venom Villa, where cobras and kraits, by the crateful, are milked of their venom before your very eyes."

"That's exciting?" said Holzman.

"The excitement comes when they get loose. There is also," I continued, "a zoo. Short on animals, true, but long on popcorn and soda pop. There's also Jolly Jungle, Parrot Paradise—''

At the next table, I noticed, sat Hedda Hasse. Solemnly sat, I might add, before a plate of untouched food. She had donned a white linen sundress that accented her dark, flowing hair. I was reminded of how Edvard Munch painted the woman who obsessed him—how her tendrils of hair reached out to choke and envelop her lover.

The singer studiously avoided my eyes, the conversation around her, and her food. She looked tense and grave. And although those classic features couldn't look anything less than lyrical, their vibrancy was stilled.

I was starting over to her when a jovial Nicholas Rouse slapped me on the back.

"Well, John," he said, "are we candidates for a murder rap, or have you already cleared us?"

"Why should I clear you? What has murder to do with me?"

"Temper, temper, John-boy! Am I complaining? Did I even say anything when you almost got us all killed yesterday?"

"You said a great deal. I heard you. I also remember your slighting remarks when I got on the plane."

"Just jokes, John. Though I wasn't too far off the mark, was I? Now I know everyone's sidestepping the issue this morning, but I think it's time we discussed it. A colleague— if not a friend—was murdered last night. The gossip this morning is that you don't think the man with the smoking revolver—if I may borrow a phrase from history—was the murderer. So saying, you have placed us all in the soup. My question is, why?"

Before I replied, I took a sip of the mucous coffee and considered. If a bad review were sufficient motive for murder, then not one of these eminent musicians could escape having a motive. We had each of us been nicked by Thorne's sharp tongue over the years. Even Lacramose the Ludicrous who, unless my eyes deceived me, was subdued and absorbed in the Help Wanted pages of the *Fun City Sun*.

As for opportunity, not a single musician had a solid alibi for the second half of the concert. I thought about this and wondered if there was any reason—beyond my own belief in them—why I should let seven likely candidates for murder scatter to the four winds.

That's where they would go, you know, these citizens of the world. All over the globe. Rouse to Berlin, Goldy to Mexico City, Holzman to one of California's everlasting festivals. All of them someplace.

With a little effort, I could prove my suspicions about the time of the murder. But to what purpose? Wasn't this murder artfully concocted to have blame fall, first, on the Marielito and, failing that, on a musician? Was I going to help a wily murderer set up one of my own?

Not on your life.

"Whether or not you know it," I said slowly, "this situation is developing into an Us Versus Them syndrome. By doing nothing—not even protesting that patent lie about Sherrill Thorne being a drug dealer—we blacken a man of honor and ourselves in the process. But by doing something, we risk—" I stopped just short of admitting that we risked placing ourselves in the pool of murder suspects and in the reach of the long arm of Florida justice, as it is called.

"Let's leave it like this," I continued. "The police are content to believe that they have Thorne's murderer, dead though he may be. I'm not happy with their conclusions, but I see no reason to dispute them until you're out of here. You all have promises to keep."

A whoop of joy went up. Amusing, when you think about it, since I had no power at all to detain them.

"There is a quid pro quo, though."

A moan swept throughout the ranks.

"I'm marooned down here with no access to the information and contacts I may need to solve this murder. I want each of you to give me your location and phone number where I can reach you. You may need to do the legwork on this case.

"One more thing," I added. "Before you leave, I want you to tell me if you've heard any gossip at all that might tie Sherrill Thorne to this place and these people. Anything that might provide a clue to why Sherrill was killed."

"Not to who killed him?" asked Freddy Rheinwein.

"Oh, we could all have killed him. Any one of us. But, aside from the irritant of an occasional bad review, we simply had no motivation. So the motivation must exist here in Fun City. Someone here must have lured Thorne down in order to kill him.''

"Couldn't they . . . he . . . she . . . simply have invited Thorne down alone for that purpose?" asked Seamus Connacht.

"Too obvious. And he wouldn't have come. I believe our presence was the murderer's cover. We were the only attraction great enough to draw Thorne down to what he called the Land of Smiles. Ironically, of course.''

"But Thorne reviewed us all the time," said Goldman.

"Never together. The last time we played together as an ensemble was for the world premiere of the Yera Concerto ten years ago. We've all gone on to solo careers since then, and I doubt if many communities could afford to bring us here for the performance of a single work. The festival sponsors seemed intent on having the original group.''

"All but you, John," pointed out Holzman. "You weren't invited.''

I took a deep breath to decimate him for this insult when he added, "Of course, I can understand why not. The last thing a murderer would want is John Field on the scent.''

Mollified, I had to admit this was true.

Everybody was rising, shuffling chairs, and drifting toward the loggia bordering Harmonia's vast interior. I shouted out one last question.

"Is anyone going directly back to New York today?"

Connacht, the leprechaun menace, reminded me that he had a recital at Alice Tully Hall the following night.

"Then you're elected," I informed him. "I want you to review the indices and microfilms of the *New York Globe* for the years that Thorne was senior critic and see if you can find any mention of these names.''

I handed the flutist a list of the balcony patrons.

"That's a terrible job," complained Seamus. "A holy fright entirely, there's no use talkin'.''

"Two hours at the most," I said. "Would you rather stay here as a murder suspect?''

He got up hastily from the table, and so did everybody else.

14

THE musicians disappeared from sight, and I was left alone with the girl of my dreams. Oblivious, it would seem, to my existence this morning.

She stayed seated at the table—as if she honestly intended to eat—and looked up at me with eyes smudged with fear and fatigue.

"You didn't tell them about the plane," she said, "and the Marielito. That forced landing wasn't your fault."

"What's the use? They'd still think so. They'd bring up other things. They'd have a point, too. Death seems to follow me around. Or do I follow death around? I've never quite figured that out."

"Tell me about it." She laughed, though her voice held no humor.

"You look terrible this morning. What's wrong?"

"Nothing. A bad night's sleep. My usual nightmares. I usually stay in your room, but it's so narrow and confined—"

"But it isn't—it's airy and magnificent."

"You should see my North Tower room. Twice as big. Anyway, that wasn't it at all. The room wasn't causing my dreams, and I should have known that. I've been having the same nightmare all my life."

"What do you dream?"

"That I'm trapped and dying. The strange part of it is that whenever I have the dream, someone does die. Again and again."

"Did you have it before our close call on the plane?"

She looked pensive and replied slowly, "No, not then. But I had it just before my parents were killed. And long before that."

"How did your parents die?"

"In a plane crash two years ago. Their own private plane got lost and came down in a blizzard. Not unusual out there. Getting around by plane is fairly common in Wyoming—because of the great distance between towns."

"That's where you're from—Wyoming?"

"My father used to teach petroleum engineering at the University of Wyoming and before that, in Lawrence. Farther east. Eventually, he went into the oil business himself, and I grew to love that part of the world. I still go back to ski there. Even though there's nothing, no one there now—"

Her eyes welled with tears, and she stopped. A more tactful man would have changed the subject then and there. But I am not a tactful man.

"About those dreams—" I began. I reached over and picked up her hands. Maybe my attention was drawn to them by the way she pointedly ignored them. "They must be quite vivid—"

I had opened her tightly closed fists. The hands were scraped and raw. They looked as though they had been soaked in water for a long time in an effort to stanch the bleeding.

"How did you do this?" I asked.

"I don't know. I must have been sleepwalking."

She withdrew her hands from mine, placed them in her lap, and gazed out at the sea to the back of beyond.

"It's a bad omen, that dream. It's always followed by sudden death. Always! That's why it frightens me so much! I'm like a Typhoid Mary—going through life unscathed while everyone around me is plucked off the planet."

I looked at her with a new awareness. "You and I have a great deal in common, you know. I just don't have the nightmares. All I can tell you is that it could be worse."

"How could it possibly be worse?"

"It could be us," I reminded her.

* * *

The sun had risen high in the heavens and was now boring down on us.

"It's after twelve," said Hedda. "Do you want to see the gardens—before it gets too hot to stroll around?"

Me turn down an invitation like that? I jumped up. With alacrity, as they say.

We sauntered from the loggia to the paths flanking the formal gardens at the rear of Harmonia. Last night, these had been an indistinguishable green blur, without form or substance. Now, from the perspective of the raised paths, I could see their formal design. Double rows of boxwood spread the entire width of the gardens, intersected by two vertical rows extending its length. At one end lay the mansion itself and at the other a baroque gazebo.

Gazebo, however, was too paltry a term for the domed and open structure framed inside by glorious, hand-painted murals. It gave an unhindered vista of the gardens and the bordering canal. Like a gazebo, though, its function was one of decoration. Or so it seemed to me.

"Is this ever used?" I asked as we approached.

"It's being used tonight. A small dinner party for the board members. That was scheduled for last night—part of the dedication hoopla for the big givers—but the events of the evening interfered. Mr. Yera felt that the balcony sponsors didn't get their $300,000 worth, so he suggested they come over this evening for a private affair. Tony is such a gracious man."

"Hmmm, yes," I said. "The oft-married Antonio Saul Yera must indeed be a charmer."

"What's wrong with that? My grandmother was married three times herself. Do you still believe in monogamy—in this day and age?"

I was going to make some flip remark about monogamy being fine for the home but that, in the office, I liked white pine. I mean, ask a stupid question, et cetera, et cetera. But a sight from the gazebo distracted me.

The canal below us looked just like swimming holes looked when I was a boy: deep, refreshing, clear as crystal. But perilously close to the canal—I rubbed my eyes. Surely it was my eyes or the hot sun or—

"Do you see what I think I see?" I asked, aghast.

Hedda followed the direction of my eyes.

"Oh, you mean the crocodiles!"

"Indeed I do."

"They're an endangered species, you know. That's just a small preserve."

"My God. Do they swim in that canal?"

"Of course not. Can't you see the steel gates?" She peered more closely. "I don't think there are more than five or six in there at the moment."

"Oh, well, only five or six—am I supposed to be relieved? Why does Yera keep them around at all?"

"He's a concerned environmentalist. And he told me once that they tend to discourage break-ins."

"Yes," I conceded. "They would."

We did a couple more turns around the park, so to speak, with Hedda pointing out the flowering poinciana trees with their bright scarlet faces raised to the skies, and I noticing the subtler and infinitely lovelier mauve blossoms of the thriving jacarandas. My companion showed me the dark mangrove trees bordering the maundering canal and told me how the trees are not trees at all but densely clustered shrubs whose shallow roots take sustenance from the water and eventually form islands upon it.

All this was moderately interesting, though it shed no light on the question that consumed me: What were Hedda's relations with the composer? Finally, I decided to put the question to her as smoothly and unobtrusively as possible.

"What," I asked offhandedly, "are your relations with Antonio Saul Yera?"

She looked at me as if I were, as P. G. Wodehouse put it, pure padded cell from the foundations up.

"What on earth do you mean?" she countered in tones that would send small boys off to the garden to eat worms. And I was perilously close to the gardens.

"Relations—" I lucidly stammered. "Do you and Yera have . . . Are you . . . Do you?" I let the thoughts drift and die on the salt air, but not before they managed to raise a few welts.

"Relations?" she asked. "Oh, you mean relatives." Graciously, and with no sign of having taken offense, she dug me out of my own hole. "Everybody's related to Mr. Yera, it seems. Even the Argentos are third cousins twice removed, or something like that. And many people think I'm Latin, because I speak the language and I have the Hispanic coloring. Actually, I'm of German-Irish heritage, like so many from the Midwest.''

"How did you come to speak Spanish?''

"Crash course here in Fun City. You have to speak Spanish to sell real estate. It's odd you should ask me about my relationship with Tony. Sherrill Thorne asked almost the same question.

"He came right out and asked you that?'' No one could ever deny that Sherrill was a curious gossip, but he was also a gentleman at all times. It wasn't like him to ask a blunt question directly.

"Yes. I was surprised and embarrassed. Then I realized he didn't mean anything offensive''—the hell he didn't—''and that he must have heard me speaking Spanish to Miguel Ochelly and concluded I was another cousin.''

"Miguel Ochelly is another cousin of Antonio Yera's? I thought he was from Colombia.''

"No, he's a Salvaniguan, like Tony. He spends a lot of time in Colombia because I believe he has business interests there.''

I'll bet he does, I thought.

"Exceedingly profitable interests,'' I said aloud, "if he can give $300,000 to an arts center.''

"Miguel gave half a million, I hear. Really commendable, considering the only singer he listens to is Lullio Gelasius.''

"Never heard of him.''

"Really? He's very big down here.''

The heat was really oppressive now. I ushered the singer to a stone bench and then flopped down beside her.

"Do you think,'' I said, fanning myself, "you could wangle an invitation for me to that dinner party tonight?''

"Why would you want to go to that?''

I looked at the dark beauty beside me. Everything about her was ambiguous. Her profession, her loyalties, even her appearance. An enigma. She had the complexion of a Latin— or the black Irish—either way you wanted to look at her. And I wanted to look at her. Far too long. I roused myself to answer her question.

"Everybody else has left. I have no excuse to stay here any longer, but I have to know these people better. One of them is a murderer, and I intend to find out which one. Of course, we don't tell them that. I need a plausible reason for staying—but not that one. Think of something."

She pondered a long time. Even her answer, uttered at last, seemed reluctantly given.

"Use real estate," she said. "Let that be your schtick. I'll drop some hints that you're interested in buying property here."

"Here?" I spoke a little too loudly. "Are you out of your mind? Why would I want to buy *here?"*

"We *tell* them that!" she flared. "I'll suggest that you're thinking about buying but that you're still undecided. You'll be amazed at how welcome you'll suddenly be on Key Cohen."

"What about Antonio Yera? Will he be willing to put up with an inquisitive guest for a couple of days?"

"I'll take care of Tony."

I didn't know just what she meant by that. And I didn't have a chance to find out, either. For Hedda rose abruptly from the bench and made straight for the slight, stooped figure of Antonio Yera.

As I watched, their figures met on the steps of Harmonia and they embraced.

Like two lovers.

15

OH, what a beautiful morning!
Oh, what a rotten P.M.!

Left in the lurch, as I was, I waited until the two lovebirds disappeared inside, then doubled back to the courtyard and took the small lift up to my room. The trip up didn't help my spirits rise accordingly.

Although the elevator's interior was executed in dark walnut panels—all hand-carved and exquisitely conceived, to be sure—it was, from a passenger's point of view, a little like ascending to heaven in a coffin.

Before the shake of a dead lamb's tail, I had come to my floor and stepped into the somewhat larger coffin of a hall. No expense had been spared there to duplicate the look of a dark, dank medieval castle, even to crumbling walls in one spot.

I was just stepping into my room when the thought struck me that I had here a unique opportunity to examine Thorne's room, directly opposite from mine.

Naturally, I tried the door to his room. Naturally, it was locked. But the solution was not hard to come by: I had the complete set of keys to Harmonia.

Someplace.

Didn't I also mention that I'm absent-minded? Quite true. That said, I must now admit that I searched everywhere for those keys. I did find, in the course of my search, the key to the night table drawer. Tucked, quite logically, in the toe of the left shoe worn at last night's performance. In time, I felt sure, the keyring would reveal itself in an equally logical location.

In the meantime, I took the key from my shoe, unlocked the table, and withdrew the contents of the night table drawer.

These had begun to receive my undivided attention when a knock at the door disturbed me.

"Yes?" If I sounded irritated, that's because I was.

"Mistah Field," said an unmistakable voice, "can ah see you foah a minute?"

Sure enough. Constanze Weber, chairman of the board. Had to be.

I swooped everything back into the drawer, slipped the key in my pocket, and opened the door for her. A waft of French perfume—musky, dark, and aromatic—preceded her. I sniffed the air.

"Y'all like it?" she asked. "It's called 'Tempetueux.' Brand-new scent from Paris. Cost a ton of money. How do you like your room, Mistah Field?" she asked, swooping right on into it. "That's a genuine Tabriz on the floor, you know. Handmade. From Iran. You'd pay the earth for it now, if you could get it at all. Ah told Tony he should hang it on the wall where people couldn't get their dirty shoes on it."

Hastily, I took my dirty shoes off it.

"Was there . . . something?" I asked with as cold a tone as I could muster. Normally, I am not averse to strange women tapping on my bedroom door. If it's not asking too much, though, I'd like them reasonably attractive and this side of sixty.

"Ah just happened to bump into Hedda when I was supervisin' the arrangements for our little get-together tonight. She said somethin' about y'all wantin' a house down here."

With the speed of light, she pressed into my hand a card reading:

CONSTANZE WEBER
PRESIDENT
FUN-IN-THE-SUN REAL ESTATE, INC.
FEEL IT LIKE A NATIVE

For all the delicacy of her long nose, I suspected Connie Weber could search out a prospective buyer as a hog sniffs out truffles. She would have, I feared, no trouble at all distinguishing between a serious buyer and a tire-kicker, as I believe the phrase goes. I had once attempted to buy a town house in Greenwich Village, and I shall never forget the ruthless interrogation an otherwise mild-mannered realtor put me through, a process he explained—when all danger had passed and we had gone out together for a drink—as "qualifying the buyer." Heaven only knew the torments that the likes of a Connie Weber could devise in that process. And she plunged right in to lay bare my soul.

"Well, Mr. Field, how much of your savings are you prepared to invest?" As a question, this could only be called point-blank. Like a bullet.

Since the whole point of this little ruse about my buying property at the end of the earth was to get these suspects talking injudiciously, I hedged somewhat on my reply. To be honest, I lied.

"Price, you understand, is no object at all. Perhaps a condominium would meet my needs, but I think I'd prefer a house. Something on the order of Harmonia, but a little more intimate, if you get my meaning. What concerns me, though—and I say this to give no offense—is the quality of life down here. Is it always like it was last night?"

She hooted—a most unbecoming hoot—and assured me that, aside from an occasional off night, Fun City was Arcadia itself.

"You seem to like it here," I continued. "Have you lived here long?"

"Over twenty years. I'm sure you'll find that hard to believe, considerin'."

"Considering what?"

"Considerin'," she simpered, "that ah don't look old enough for that."

"For what?"

"Ah came down to Fun City when the first Cuban refugees did—but from a different direction. Georgia," she confided, "is my home."

"Were you in real estate there, too?"

"In Georgia? Oh, no. No indeed. Keeping body and soul

together was about all I could manage in the land of my birth.
I didn't mean I came here directly from Georgia. There was
many a slip between the cup and the—''

She stopped abruptly, looked at me narrowly, and placed
the ball neatly in my court.

"But let's talk about you, Mr. Field. I'm sure my firm—
either myself or one of my salespersons—can help you. We
have multiple listin's on every property offered for sale in Fun
City. And I have a complete lock on the market in Key Cohen. You work through us, and you'll get the best buy in
town!''

Gone was the charm and vagueness that had marked all
her previous remarks. I looked into the cold eyes of a successful businesswoman, and it was very much like looking
into the barrel of a gun.

"Uh—'' I said brightly, casting about for a lifeline, ''what
are multiple listings?''

Out came the southern accent again, along with a tinkling
laugh that rippled up and down two octaves.

"Oh, Mistah Field, you must foahgive me! Everybody—
but everybody—talks real estate in Florida, so ah just assumed you'd understand our lingo.''

From her Olympian heights, she placed a firm hand on my
shoulder and pushed me down on a pretty good imitation of
a Louis XV chaise longue.

"I'll be glad to give you a crash course,'' she breathed.

"In real estate?''

"That, too.''

There ensued a life-and-death struggle in which the thought
rose, forlornly, that if this was known as qualifying the buyer
in Florida, I was willing to settle for questions. Suddenly, the
phone rang on the table next to us, and—like a drowning man
bobbing to the surface for the third time—I put out a limp
hand to grasp Ma Bell's lifesaver.

It was Hedda. "Is Connie Weber there?''

Judging from the hundred sixty pounds encircling me like
an octopus, I would have said so, but my breath was coming
in gasps now. I found it hard to speak.

Connie grabbed the phone. From my worm's-eye view—
pinned under by the sheer weight of the real estate tycoon—I
gathered that Hedda had just received a call from a recal-

citrant buyer who was threatening to withdraw from a sale.
Her boss proceeded to give her a few tips on how to avert
that disaster.

"You tell him we'll take him to court, honey. . . . He's
going to lose more than his deposit money on this one. . . .
Tell him he can go to jail for five years if he backs out now."

As the old adage says, when money comes in the door,
love goes out the window. Something like that. Connie lost
interest in me as rapidly as a dog loses interest in a bone with
no meat on it. As she went on talking to Hedda, she loosened
her hold on my shoulder.

Slowly, I emerged from the depths of the chaise longue,
virtue intact, while a preoccupied Connie informed me that
she would have to tend to Hedda's problem immediately. But
if I had any questions at all, she could answer them. Maybe
I would like Hedda to take me for a ride to see some prop-
erties?

That sounded nice, I said.

Hedda had her car right over here, she said, or she would
take me herself. In the meantime, she would speak to Hedda
about likely holdings that would grab my interest.

"You don't want anything less than a million, do you?"

"Whatever it takes," I said grandly. "What is money if it
can't buy comfort?"

We smiled in unison, and Connie made a move toward the
door. I took her by the arm and steered her over closer to it.
I then opened the door, which swung out to reveal the locked
door to Thorne's room.

"That reminds me," said Connie Weber. "Luis, the security guard, says you have all the keys to Harmonia."

"All of them? Surely there are duplicates."

"No, none at all. Tony keeps only one complete set—as a
security measure. I told Luis I'd remind you."

I started to escort her toward the tiny lift, but she shied
away from it. A severe case of claustrophobia, she said. So I
walked with her down the circular steps that opened to the
courtyard.

"By the way," I said in warm conversational tones, "did
you know Sherrill Thorne before last night?"

"A city slicker like that? Hardly, John." She giggled like
the jeune fille she thought she was. "How would a little girl

from Georgia know a big-time music critic like Sherrill Thorne?''

I could have pointed out that it was a long time since she had been little, a girl, or from Georgia. Such a lapse of charity, though, was beyond me, and I stuck to the matter at hand.

"But wasn't it you," I said, "who invited Thorne down for last night's performance?"

"Me? Why would I—well, I suppose I had to be the one to send the letter, since I was chairman of the Yera Festival. But it was someone else's suggestion. I've forgotten whose. Why do you ask?"

She paused in the hallway landing and straightened a picture on the wall. Then we went out in the courtyard, now transformed by the gathering dusk. She was fidgeting to leave and to give Hedda some timely tips on toppling timorous customers. But I dawdled near the fountain, making no reply to her question.

"Well," she prompted, "why do you want to know who asked Thorne here?"

"No real reason. It just seemed to me that whoever invited Thorne here must have known him well. Well enough to know what temptations he'd respond to. In this case, the prospect of a great performance."

"You mean—he wasn't the type of man to respond to the usual temptations of money, money, and more money?"

"Some people aren't."

"They're fools, then. Idealistic, impractical fools. Anyone who thinks he's going to change the way the world thinks is a born windmill-tilter."

"There was nothing evangelical about Thorne. He just had a healthy fear about money and what it does to people."

"Then he shouldn't have come to Fun City. You're nobody here—or anyplace else—unless you have money."

"Luckily, money is no problem for you," said I in avuncular tones. "Nor for me," I added hastily. "I'm just trying to understand the viewpoint of those who tend to put achievement first. Antonio Yera, for example, strikes me as a man who doesn't care a tap about money."

"Oh, well—Tony. He can afford to—he's old money, about the oldest in Fun City. He's had money all his life. From both sides of his family."

"Still, he's giving away a huge chunk of it by donating Harmonia to Fun City. This estate must be worth tens of millions."

"It's all very well for Tony Yera to give Harmonia to the community. Have you any idea what a tax write-off that is? We should all give away our houses and then continue to live in them for the rest of our lives." Connie Weber didn't even bother to conceal the edge of spite and jealousy in her voice. "He may be a great composer," she snapped, "but let me tell you, Tony is one sharp businessman. Not for nothing was he Solomon Schwarzkopf's grandson."

"Schwarzkopf, Schwarzkopf," I said, "where have I heard that name before? Wasn't that the—"

"The man who invented the paper clip, I'm told. You can imagine what a money-maker that's been through the years. And that's just on his mother's side. Tony's father was Trujillo Yera."

"What! The strong-arm dictator of Salvanigua? That was Antonio Saul Yera's father?"

"Didn't you know that?" She seemed genuinely surprised. "It's no secret here."

Not only did I not know it, but I doubted that Sherrill Thorne knew it, either. At least, he hadn't mentioned a word about it to me in that long biographical sketch in the plane. Probably didn't want to reveal any of the warts on his idol. Not that Yera could help who his father was. But that a passionate and outspoken liberal like Yera should be the son of the dictator who bled Salvanigua dry before his own assassination—I tell you, it boggled the mind.

"I find that hard to believe," I said. "Antonio Saul Yera has been so vocal about speaking out on the dangers of all totalitarian societies—"

"Oh yes, Tony was a young Turk in his day. Broke with his father for a while. But it was his father, after all. And time heals all wounds, you know."

Connie Weber turned to leave, and I could see there was no detaining her now. Although I had discovered a real treasure trove of information about Antonio Yera, I had learned precious little about the interviewee of this long chat. So I posed one last question to her.

"You seem to know the composer's background very well. Have you known him long?"

"Well and long, Mr. Field." Gone was the "John" of yore. We were no longer buddies.

"Hasn't anyone mentioned," she continued, "that I used to be married to Antonio Saul Yera?"

Before I managed to put my two jaws back together, Connie Weber had hurried off toward the gazebo in the distance.

16

WHEN a bombshell explodes, most people scatter. It is my unhappy lot in life to stay and assess the damage. And that is what I did. I stayed in the courtyard and thought about Connie's grenade, so casually tossed in my lap.

So Constanze Weber was the last contender for the title to Antonio Saul Yera's affections. Wives Number Three and Four, in that order. From the evidence of my own eyes, Hedda Hasse would be Wife Number Five. So what? Who was counting?

Except me, of course. That was the sticking point. Surely the heat was affecting my brain cells. Or was John Field—St. John the Austere to his friends—turning into a romantic? Falling—the words clogged in my throat—in love?

If so, it felt a lot like the flu. Depression invariably accompanies those symptoms, and I'm Irish, you know, a race not only subject to despair but tending to wallow in it. As I was wallowing now. I looked around the courtyard and noted that the folds of night were closing in fast. Dusk had almost given up. Much like myself. I was ready to go home.

And why not? Who wanted me to stay? What point in finding Thorne's murderer, when murder was a way of life down here? Who would punish Thorne's murderer—even if I found him? Who cared about it at all?

Well, I did. Fat lot of good that did me. I watched the

fountain sputtering over the hideous block of abstract sculpture. I traced with my foot the enigmatic motto in the mosaic tilework—"Music As Thy Name Is"—and recalled how ecstatic Thorne had been to discover those words just last night.

My morbidities were cut short by the arrival of one of the patrons.

"Mr. Field?" he said, extending his hand. "I'm Joseph Lange."

"Oh, yes," I said. "I know you by reputation, of course. You are the artist—"

"The artist of ecology. The earth is my palette. Have you seen any of my work?"

"I was on Norma's Vineyard shortly after you wrapped that island in swaddling."

"One of my more impressive accomplishments."

"Just before the twelve whales washed up on the beach."

"Most unfortunate. Did they ever find out what caused that?"

Now there was a conversation-stopper. Environmentalists, as we all know, thrive in New England, and to this day they thirst for the blood of Joseph Lange. They had warned of the consequences if Lange were permitted to stage his "painting"—acres and acres of chemically treated white sheets enveloping the shorelines. Specifically, they stated that marine life would suffer.

Lange had pooh-poohed their protests and barreled ahead with his project, with orchestration from the media. The result was twelve dead whales and a dearth of edible fish for Boston for some months. But the publicity was invaluable. Lange's earth paintings brought him glory.

As I mentioned earlier, Lange had a head too big for his small body. I will now go further. Lange had a head so big, it could be mounted and stuffed. Only the antlers were missing, but the masses of long hair—jutting off at odd points—more or less served that purpose. He had the dark, soulful eyes and the olive complexion of a Latin. I remembered that Antonio Yera had referred to him as a distant cousin, a relationship one would not guess from the painter's German surname.

Lange got down to business in no time.

"I hear you're looking for property in Fun City."

"Word travels fast here."

Lange's eyes—soulful as they were—had a disconcerting habit of landing on you and then skidding off at an angle. They sideswiped you. I saw that he had fastened his glance at a point somewhere above my head. The three windows of the South Tower engaged him totally and provided me a good detour from real estate.

"That's the Madame de Pompadour Room," I said, pointing to the first window. "That's where I am. Interesting architecture, don't you think?"

"Ummm. Who's occupying the North Tower?"

"I believe Ms. Hasse has that."

He cast his eyes—narrowly escaping mine—in that direction.

"The North Tower is much more interesting architecturally. One sweeping room. Lots of light. Marvelous panorama of the bay. The South Tower rooms are much too cut up. That's something you should consider in your house quest, Mr. Field. Consider the flow."

"Flow?"

"Go with the flow," he advised.

With that, he pressed into my hand a small card reading:

JOSEPH LANGE
ARTIST/REAL ESTATE BROKER
LANGE ENTERPRISES, INC.
CREATIVE LIVING THROUGH CREATIVE HOUSING

"You look surprised," he said. "Didn't I mention I also sell houses?"

"Doesn't everyone?"

"My specialty is homes that meet the creative needs of people like ourselves—"

"How creative?"

"—homes that begin at $500,000 and end—"

"In bankruptcy?" I suggested.

He smiled a thin smile and assessed the cut of my blue blazer. It met the test, and I hesitated to mention that it was borrowed.

"Naturally, the money is of small concern to me," I said breezily and even honestly. Money *is* of small concern if you haven't got it. My fees are large and respectable, mind you, but the public at large has no idea how small they are compared to those of, say, a corporate lawyer. Such is the fate of people who do what they really want to do.

"—and while I do need something in that price range," I continued, "or above," I threw in, "I am rather pressed for time."

Lange trembled like an Irish setter who had just caught a bone.

"I'm sure we can find something for you quickly. The important thing is that you work with someone *sympathique* to your needs. How soon do you have to get back?"

"My next engagement is in Paris on Wednesday. But if there's time, I'd like to accompany Sherrill Thorne's body to New York."

A tiny shudder rippled through his tiny shoulders. He looked around the open courtyard, as if Thorne's ghost were lurking in the shadows, ready to pounce on him.

"Just think," he said in a strained voice, "he was right here among us last night. Here today, gone tomorrow. A tragic affair, wasn't it? But you mustn't let what happened turn you against Fun City."

"Did you know Sherrill Thorne?" I asked.

For just a fraction of a second, Lange's eyes looked straight into mine, and I saw their look of terror.

"No! I never knew him!"

"But you just said you saw him right here last night."

"I came late, you'll recall. I wasn't even in the receiving line. True, I saw him here and recognized him, but after that snide remark when he used *me* as a metaphor—"

"When was that?"

"Ages ago. I've forgotten the exact words." He then proceeded to give me the exact words. "He said, 'Anton Stoll directs large choirs like Joseph Lange devises earth paintings: abominably.'"

"An unfortunate comparison," I said. "Still—" I was going to say, "Have you ever *heard* Stoll?" and caught my tongue just in time.

"Still," I said, "you surely wanted to confront him about that insult. I would. Didn't you meet him along with the other patrons at intermission?"

Again, that look of terror. And when he spoke, finally, his voice shook.

"Yes, I talked to him a few minutes then. I was roped into that."

"By whom?"

"I have no idea. It was just one of those things one *had* to do. I mumbled my name to him, and he acted as if he'd never heard of me. I couldn't have exchanged five words with him."

"What did you say?"

"Just the usual garbage—how splendid of him to review the performance. Particularly hypocritical in my case."

"Do you remember what he said to you?"

The diminutive painter placed two well-manicured hands over his ears, as if he wished to shut out all memory of what he'd heard in Thorne's box.

"No! It was impossible! I know I imagined it. He didn't say anything—really he didn't!"

"What do you think he said?"

"I heard a whisper! That's all! A whisper! There were so many people in that box that I couldn't have heard a whisper. . . . That's why I know I imagined it . . . after . . . everything . . . happened."

The wind must have blown a stone loose overhead. There was a slight sound in the gallery above us. In the still silence, it seemed louder than it was. Like an echo.

"Who's there?" cried Lange. "Is that you, Bobby?"

I searched for face or form and saw nothing.

"There's no one there," I said. "It's just the wind. Tell me what you heard Thorne say."

"All right! All right!" The painter had removed his hands from his ears and was now wringing them. His hands, I mean. "I have to tell someone, or I'll go out of my mind!

"In the middle of my little spiel, while I was going on about how wonderful it was to have him here—and really, I couldn't have cared less—he leaned over and whispered something in my ear."

Again, Lange hesitated and peered out into the darkness.

"Yes, yes. Go on. You must have heard him very clearly."

"I couldn't have. What he said—what I thought he said—

was . . . was''—Lange's voice took on the tone and color of
Thorne's own—

'' 'Get me out of here!' ''

And this time I heard something, too.

The quick intake of breath from an unseen observer.

No doubt about it now.

On the open gallery directly above us, quick footsteps were
heard retreating along the balcony. Audible on the tiles.

"Who's there?" I called out. For answer, I heard the sound
of a heavy door closing. Of the ten or so doors opening off
the gallery balcony, it could have been any one. Too dark to
see.

I started toward the steps leading to the balcony when the
courtyard was suddenly flooded with light.

"What are you two doing out here in the dark?" asked an
approaching Adonis. "Why didn't you turn on the lights?"

A relieved Lange greeted the blond giant with unfeigned
enthusiasm. Then he placed an arm through the Viking's
crooked elbow and dragged him over in my direction.

"Mr. Field, may I present Robert O'Reilly. A musician
like yourself. And a lawyer, as well."

"We met briefly," Robert O'R. reminded me, "at the pre-
concert reception."

"Thank God it's you," breathed Lange.

"Of course it's me. What are you talking about? I've been
looking all over for you, Joseph. Don't you know the party's
starting at the belvedere?"

"What belvedere?"

"The gazebo, darling. *Gazebo* doesn't do it justice. *Belvedere*—meaning 'beautiful view'—does."

"Bobby knows Italian," explained the painter. "Bobby
knows everything."

"Most everything, Joseph." Bobby whipped out a comb
and, from his mirrored reflection in the fountain, touched up
his errant locks. "What I don't know is what the belvedere
has a beautiful view of—except crocodiles. Those I find
frightening to behold. But that's beside the point. The point
being that the tables are all set up for dinner, and I've been
dispatched to round up all the patrons. Are you a patron, Mr.
Field?"

The question was rhetorical, but the tone was rude. I drew myself up to deliver an appropriate squelcher when Lange intervened.

"Mr. Field is much better than a patron, Bobby. He's a prospect."

"For real estate," I amended. (Not all the crocodiles were in that pit.)

Robert O'Reilly looked down at his toes—like a peacock—and screeched.

"Oh, you must forgive me! I'm so sorry! I had no idea! How thoughtless of me!"

Lange sent him telepathic signals through the night air. "Perhaps you'd wish to—"

Quick as lightning, O'Reilly thrust forward an engraved card proclaiming him a lawyer, *the* lawyer, for Lange Enterprises, Inc.

"My field of specialization," he informed me, "is real estate. But I can handle anything—wills, divorces, property settlements—anything at all where money is involved. Just remember, I'm here to serve you."

"Did I understand Mr. Lange to say that you are also a musician?"

"I try to keep my hand in. I started out as a professional musician. In New York."

"Really? Did you ever meet Sherrill Thorne when you were playing professionally?"

O'Reilly laughed wryly.

"We never met—not face to face. But he did enough damage in a single review to turn my footsteps in another direction."

"What do you mean?"

"He reviewed my debut recital at Town Hall, Mr. Field. I play the krummhorn,* you know, and I like to think I am a virtuoso of that instrument."

"Didn't Thorne agree?"

"He did not." O'Reilly's handsome features darkened in

---

* A woodwind instrument sounded by an enclosed double reed, employed principally in the sixteenth and seventeenth centuries. Now that early music devotees are multiplying at the speed of sound—especially in Boston—the krummhorn is being duplicated by instrument makers.

memory. Not a pretty sight. "He had the gall to write that if what I played was early music, we should all be grateful that time marches on."

"Cruel."

"Heinous, actually. You can understand why I turned to law after that. Happily, though, the pleasures of the krumm-horn will never be entirely lost to me. I have a few students at Suntan U. I practice daily. And I play for friends. That is what music is all about. Emotional satisfaction. Wasn't it Frederick the Great who expressed it so well? He learned that a friend—or a courtier—or a prince—"

"Somebody like that," I prompted.

"—didn't play an instrument, and he said to him, 'What will you do in your old age?'"

"Ah, but you, Bobby," said Lange, "you will never grow old. Never."

"I don't intend to." O'Reilly ran a graceful hand across an unruly blond lock with very dark roots. "We've cornered the market on plastic surgeons down here. But come along, both of you. Soup's on in the belvedere."

As we started our trek through the formal gardens of Harmonia, Bobby drew me aside for some confidential advice.

"There's a minefield of realtors out there," he warned. And his voice took on a menacing tone.

"If I were you, I'd watch my step."

17

FROM afar, we could see the party was warming up. Shrieks of laughter exploded as regularly as champagne corks, and the sounds were wafted along on the night breeze.

I sauntered slowly and tried to elicit from Lange and O'Reilly any information they might have on Thorne and his Fun City connections. They insisted they hadn't the foggiest.

"One thing, John—I may call you John, mayn't I?" said O'Reilly. "I had nothing to do with inviting Sherrill Thorne down here, and I can't imagine who did. Mind you, a Yera Festival is long overdue, but the town is far from ready for judgment from out-of-town critics."

"Did you talk to Thorne at all?"

"No. I even avoided him at the reception."

"You didn't go into his box at intermission?"

"I did not. Tony Yera asked me to. I smiled pleasantly and said yes. But I had no intention of chatting with a man I could have cheerfully murdered."

Lange halted and glowered at the lawyer.

"He didn't mean that, Mr. Field. Bobby speaks in hyperbole. Exaggerates everything—you should see him in court. Bobby, Mr. Field is the famous John Field—"

"I know that. I have several of his records."

"—the DETECTIVE." Lange spoke in all caps.

"So?" asked the imperturbable Robert. "Is that supposed

116

to frighten me? Am I to gather that you don't buy our police commissioner's neat solution of the murder?''

"It is somewhat far-fetched," I allowed.

"Ah, you're a cynic. You really should live here. Well, I wish you luck in your efforts to right a wrong. But I can't imagine who in Fun City would want to kill Sherrill Thorne. Besides myself, that is. There must be scads of people in New York City. Besides yourself, that is.''

O'Reilly placed his hands on his forehead, the better to focus on the scene ahead.

"I see the waiters are still setting up tables,'' he said, "and I don't smell the food yet. That gives me time for a cigarette, a verboten luxury around our esteemed composer.''

"He does seem to feel strongly on the subject," I agreed.

"We were virtually frisked for lighters and matches when we walked in last night. And I'm not exaggerating, Joseph. Don't say I am. That, by the way, is what I was doing during intermission last night, when I should have been offering obeisance to Thorne. I was lighting up like a smokestack out on the patrons' terrace.''

"All by yourself?''

"To tell you the truth, I'm not sure. I had the sense someone was with me in the darkness. Gave me the willies. Dedicated smoker that I am, though, I still puffed as long as possible and zipped up to our box just as the lights were going down.''

"Did you run into anyone in the hallway?''

"Not a soul. It was lonely as a crypt up there.''

Lange started to accompany me to the gazebo, but Bobby warned him against it.

"Don't you see who's hiding in the bushes?''

"Who?'' asked I, in alarm.

"The charming Alicia Argento and her sinister spouse. The next in a long line of part-time realtors. You don't mind if we sit this one out?''

Sitting this one out was what I had in mind, but it was not to be. Madame Argento emerged from the shadows and greeted me like Penelope welcoming Odysseus back from his travels. Just my luck that Armando was also on the home-coming committee.

Alicia was straining the seams of a form-fitting gold lamé gown that shimmered and shook with every breath.

"Oh, Meester Feeld," she squealed, sending shock waves rippling through every thread. "I'm so glad you're staying with us a few days longer. Ees eet true that you are going to buy property here?"

"I'm considering it," I allowed. "Why? Do you sell real estate?"

"Mostly to our compatriots. There are so many of us here. We try to limit our business to ex-ambassadors."

"That many, are there?"

"Eet only works for a leetle while. Then all the diplomats get real estate licenses, and the competition eet gets cut-throat."

"May I speak undiplomatically?" I asked. "Does every-body in Florida sell real estate?"

The doe-eyed beauty batted her long eyelashes and consid-ered the question.

"My third cousin twice removed arrived in thees country two weeks ago. She does not sell real estate. Yet."

"You forget about me, my dear," said the hovering Ar-gento. "I spend but a small portion of my time selling prop-erty."

"And the rest of your time?" I asked.

"The rest of my time I spend molding American public opinion."

"Really? In any particular direction?"

"Toward the freedom of Salvanigua, the downing of ty-rants, the restitution of lands to their rightful owners, and the full commitment of American troops to this noble enter-prise."

"That doesn't leave much time for selling houses, I sup-pose. Are you getting much help from your friends?"

"Tremendous support. Antonio Yera, whose father's sis-ter's second husband's son by his first marriage was married to my aunt's great-nephew's daughter, has been the soul of generosity to his countrymen."

"How do you mean? Money?"

"Money, of course, is invaluable. Both in setting up training grounds and in, uh, apprising, uh, certain U.S. Senators of Salvanigua's plight.''

In a sharp voice at odds with her soft curves, Alicia Argento broke into our dialogue, with no apologies at all.

"Armando!" she said—as one would say "Fido!"—"I think it's time we joined the rest of the guests. Everybody is waiting for us. In your house-hunting, Meester Feeld, you weel remember me. Won't you?"

I assured her that I would never forget her. She placed her real estate card more or less between my teeth and sadly relinquished me to the next shark in line.

That would be Frieda Sweeten.

In her sweet little Alice-blue gown, she looked no less formidable than she had last night. The tiara helped, of course, as well as the vivid red hair. She looked a lot like Bette Davis playing Elizabeth I about thirty years too late.

I fully expected a regal approach to real estate salesmanship, but her method was downright folksy. Proving, once again, you never can tell.

Right off, Frieda launched into the advantages of Florida as a retirement community. This to a man who had only recently dipped his feet into his thirties.

"Sneak up on you before you know it! Old age, I mean. But the wonderful thing about Florida is that you always feel young."

"How's that?"

"No matter how old you are, there's always someone down the block much older than you. Take my mother, for example—"

"Your mother is—is—is still among us?"

"Ninety-seven and going strong. Just found the perfect house for her, too. I told her that two acres was plenty for her to handle at her age. Got a good buy for her, too. Even gave her a break on my commission."

"Wonderful," I said.

"I mean, what is family for?"

In the spirit of good fellowship, she plunged a bony elbow in my ribs. Immediately, I doubled over and began coughing.

"What you need is a good drink! What'll it be?"

"Scotch," I gasped.

"You stay right there," she said, "and don't move a muscle."

How could I? I was paralyzed and choking to death. I could sense, rather than see, the gathering hordes of realtors moving in on me for the kill. Frieda cut them down as a scythe mows wheat.

"He's mine!" she said to the crowd at large. "You can all have a crack at him after dinner, but it's my turn now. Freddy, you keep this young man safe from our friends."

With that, Frieda swept off, and the crowd parted just as it would for Butch Cassidy.

Or should I say—for Good Queen Bess?

18

GENERAL Vance Sweeten came running, as a well-trained husband should. He drew up a chair, adjusted it, and addressed his remarks into the faceless void of the night.

"John Field, isn't it?" he said to an oleander tree.

"Yes, I'm John Field."

The sound of my voice turned him around, roughly in my direction.

"A great pleasure, my dear sir. I didn't realize it was you in the receiving line. But I knew it was you up there last night. Knew it the moment you played the first note on the piano. Even though I couldn't read the program or see you clearly, I knew it had to be John Field. That clarity of thought and that richness of tone. Had to be you."

I was dumbfounded. "You're very kind," I said.

"Kindness has nothing to do with it. Am I right—or did you have to transpose the piano up a whole tone?"

I looked at him with new respect. Someone in the audience had picked that up? Knew about the crisis onstage?

"How did you know?" I asked.

"When you ran your fingers up and down the keyboard before the performance. Knew the piano was off-pitch by a whole tone. Thought sure our high-priced ensemble of world-class performers was going to have to switch to a Strauss waltz then and there. Wasn't that what the conductor was conducting, by the way?''

"We think so. We're not sure. He may just have been trying to stay warm, so cold was the wave of panic up on that stage.''

"Well, the show went on,'' said Sweeten, "thanks to you. I know of only one comparable achievement in the annals of music, and yours exceeded that.'' He then cited—in accurate detail—the legendary feat of pianism performed by Johannes Brahms during a tour with the Hungarian violinist Reményi. At sight, Brahms transcribed Beethoven's Violin Sonata in C minor to C-sharp minor.

"In fact,'' he concluded, "the entire evening would have been a total triumph. Except for the murder. Horrible. Horrible thing. Quite beyond belief.''

"Had you met Sherrill Thorne before last night?''

"Just once,'' he said. "At the wedding.''

I waited. The old man did not elucidate, so I was forced to prod.

"What wedding was that?''

"Oh, Frieda's sister's. She was married to Thorne. Dead now.''

"How did she die?'' I asked.

"Automobile accident. Thorne was driving. Eleanor was trapped in the car and burned to death. Thorne was thrown clear.''

"So that's why he would never drive a car. I knew his wife had died, but I never knew the circumstances. He worshipped her, you know. Never married again. Always spoke of her as if she were still alive.''

"You'd have a hard time convincing my wife of that. Frieda never forgave him. Between us,'' he leaned over to whisper, "Frieda always thought Thorne was responsible for her sister's death. Usually, it's the passenger who's thrown clear and the driver who's trapped. Anyway the man always drove like a maniac.

"Good thing they caught Thorne's murderer,'' added Sweeten. "Otherwise, I wouldn't put it past Frieda. She always said she'd kill Sherrill Thorne herself if she ever got the chance. That's why we didn't even go and visit him at intermission. Wouldn't be surprised if she didn't put a time bomb in there. She's quite a woman!''

He laughed heartily, still chuckling when Frieda returned bearing two drinks. With these new insights to her character, she took on added dimensions, petite though she was.

"Nothing for you, old man," she said to her husband. "Bad for you."

"Jesus!" shouted Sweeten.

Jesus appeared with a tray of champagne cocktails. Handed the aged general a glass of the bubbly and departed. But not before the muscled Colombian Miguel Ochelly grabbed a glass off the tray and lingered to chat.

"General Sweeten speaks Spanish fluently, you know," he said. "When he chooses to. He knows that the name Jesus is pronounced *'Ha-sus'* in our language and that our aspirate J is far more pleasing to the ear than the harsh English J."

"Whaddya mean 'our' language? Where do you think you are, anyway?" Sweeten's manner was so rude, I felt pity for the inoffensive Ochelly. Who had a better command of English than I had been led to believe, by the way.

"Listen to this crowd!" roared the old man. At the time, he was addressing the crocodiles in the pit, but I dimly discerned that he referred to the people behind him.

The buzz of Spanish enveloped us on all sides. Even Hedda was carrying on in Spanish over in a corner with Antonio Yera.

"Talk English, Tony!" yelled the general to the crocodiles. The composer looked up momentarily and smiled at us indulgently.

"In my day," said Sweeten, "men showed young women their etchings. Not Tony. He makes them listen to recordings. At least, that's what he's trying to do now."

Vance Sweeten's hearing really *was* remarkable. Yera's table was a good ten feet away, and Sweeten was even facing in the opposite direction. With some effort, I removed my gluelike glance from Hedda and fastened it onto the general, and whatever it was he was trying to say. Oh, yes. Music.

"One goes with one's strong suit," I said. "In Mr. Yera's case, that would be his own music. Maybe not sentimental. Simply glorious."

"Oh, that's not what he plays for his ladies!" Sweeten

laughed loudly at the idea. "No, he plays old recordings of the late and great singer George Carlos Mayor. Much more romantic!"

"Debatably great and debatably romantic," I said. "Why him?"

"The effect is said to be mesmerizing," said Ochelly. "Many times, I have been on the point of borrowing those records myself. But then," he added modestly, "it really hasn't been necessary in my case."

And he was right. He didn't even have to whistle. Connie Weber materialized from the crowd to place a proprietary arm on Ochelly.

"Connie!" said Sweeten, his face wreathed in smiles. He turned around and held up his cheek for an appropriate greeting. "Still wearing that godawful perfume but looking, I daresay, like Helen of Troy!"

Only, I thought, if Helen of Troy were tall, but I forget that beauty is in the eye of the beholder. Particularly if the beholder is blind.

"You are a cahd, Vance!" said the face that, in her day, launched a thousand ships. At least. "Isn't he a cahd, Mistah Field? Bet he's been telling y'all about his pet peeves. How the city is changin', how nobody speaks English here anymore, about the wreckage of our beautiful countryside—"

"Well, he's right about that, Connie," said Frieda defensively. "If it hadn't been for Vance and the rest of us here, there'd be an elevated bullet train running through Key Cohen right now. Progress, indeed!"

"Really?" I said, in the tone of a concerned homeowner who has just learned the identity of the winged creatures abounding along the floorboards. "Any chance of that actually happening?"

"No chance at all," assured Frieda, "now that we've all kicked up such a fuss. There was a threat about a year or so ago that the county would take this land on Key Cohen by the right of eminent domain."

"Why?" I asked, the picture of concern.

"Because Key Cohen's on the highest land in the county, and it's the most direct route to the southern half of Fun City. The county proposed to build two bridges to the mainland, tear down Harmonia, and run the line right through this beautiful island. Would have wrecked the resale potential of every house over here.''

''How did you stop them?''

Frieda Sweeten chuckled with sweet satisfaction.

''Only thing that saved us,'' she said, ''is that we got Harmonia designated as a historical monument.''

''Isn't it only about twenty years old?''

''That's older than anything else around here—excepting me and Vance and you, too, Connie! But to really clinch it, we talked Tony Yera into donating Harmonia to the city as an arts center.''

''Now, Frieda,'' began the realtor, ''you know Tony intended to do that all along.''

''Sure he did. But after he died. That could be years from now.''

An embarrassed silence followed. And about time. It must have dawned on everyone that they had revealed a good deal of dirty linen for a stranger to examine. This small band had successfully undermined a transportation project in the name of art and real estate values. As an added fillip, they had just revealed a touching lack of concern for their friend Antonio Yera, whom rumor and the evidence of one's eyes already had at death's door. But for them, he couldn't die quick enough.

Some comment was expected from me. So I tried to place myself in the frame of mind of a passing millionaire whose investment was going to be, thanks be to God, safe after all. A homeowner anxious to fit in with the neighbors.

''It's a good thing,'' I said, ''there are a few high-minded people down here who think of the future.''

Then I added, with a bright smile, ''Aren't they starting to serve dinner now?''

Once again, I drew the short straw. Hedda Hasse was not my dinner partner. I got to break bread with Rachael Radler, an impressive dinner partner in terms of size, and with Lisa DaPonto, a woman in this world but not of it, if you know what I mean. The only antidote was that Vance Sweeten would complete the foursome, and I did enjoy the old man's company. One doesn't often get to sit down to dinner with a World War II legend.

General Sweeten, it turned out, had known the Yera family in Salvanigua some sixty years before, when he—Sweeten—was a young military attaché assigned to the American Embassy.

"Hilo wasn't always a dictator, you know." First I knew that Trujillo Yera, that strong-arm terrorist, ever was young enough or human enough to have a nickname.

"When I knew him," continued Sweeten, "he was simply a young Army officer doing his best for his country and his family. He didn't have then the power that corrupted him later. Antonio was just a young boy of ten or eleven. Unquestionably gifted, musically. Even then, I thought he'd be an outstanding performer. He had had that outgoing personality that thrives on praise. Fearless in front of an audience. I remember that performing was second nature to him—he loved to do it."

"Were you surprised that he became such a distinguished composer?"

"No. I was surprised that he turned to it relatively late in life. But Tony always had that serious streak to his nature. Even when I lost track of him, during his Broadway hiatus, I always knew he'd return to serious music."

"Did you think it would be quite so serious?"

"What? Oh, you mean the quality of his compositions?"

"Yes. Considering that he'd made his name in a much lighter genre—Broadway musicals."

"Well, it just shows you," said Sweeten, "that tragedy sometimes shapes our lives for the better—though you're too bowed down by grief to notice it at the time."

"Was it such a tragedy?" I asked. "Yera married again—his previous wife, I hear. Could he have done that if he were so grief-stricken?"

"You'd really have to ask Tony that. And I doubt if he'd tell you. I never knew any of Tony's wives—except Connie. Splendid woman. Gave us a fantastic buy here on Key Cohen. I think she's the glue that's held Tony's life together through all his troubles.

"Oh, I know all the gossip," he continued. "But I never met the pianist he fell in love with. Theresa von Trattner, wasn't it? Tony was living in New York then, estranged from his father. Family is family, to my way of thinking, and I really didn't have much to do with Tony until he moved down here and remarried his wife and settled his differences with his father. Good thing, too—his father's days were numbered. Assassinated as soon as he left Salvanigua, right here in Harmonia. That's what tipped the scales with Tony. After that, he came to peace with himself and made something out of his life. He began to compose great music.''

"Trujillo Yera was killed here?'' I was astounded. But then, dictators are always assassinated someplace. Why not here?

"He was shot right outside of the Hall of Mirrors. You can still see the machine-gun bullets in the lobby. Tony insisted on that. A reminder of what terrorism can do, he says. Myself, I think it's macabre.''

"When did all this happen?''

"A few months after the revolution. Right after the revolutionary regime released him. By then, Trujillo Yera was a physical wreck. Poor old man couldn't have hurt anybody by that time. Half-paralyzed and speechless. Far as I can see, not much was accomplished by that revolution. All they did was replace one tyrant with another.''

"It was ever thus,'' I agreed.

The general and I had been chatting, almost to the exclusion of the two women at the table. Finally, I remembered my manners and turned to Rachael Radler, on my right.

"Were you here then, Mrs. Radler?''

"When?'' she asked. "Will you pass me that sauce?''

"During the Salvaniguan revolution, when all the refugees came over?''

"Oh my, yes. Richard and I had just moved down from New York.''

"Your husband was transferred here by the bank?''

"No, Richard wasn't in banking then. He was—are we going to get any more wine? Can you signal the waiter, Mr. Field?''

I complied and pressed her further. "Your husband—you were telling me about your move to Fun City.''

She munched for a while and concentrated on her plate.

"Richard wasn't in banking then. He was . . . between . . . professions.'' This sentence was delivered between mouthfuls.

"What is a banker before he's a banker?'' It was an innocent question, but Rachael seemed not to hear it at all. A sharp kick on my shin—my left shin—was a clear signal from the silent Lisa DaPonto to cease and desist. So I did.

"The important thing," said the local impresario, "is what he is now. As a banker, he can be a big help in financing your property purchase. And as a realtor, I can help you find just the house you need. The important thing is not to get committed to anyone else."

She slid two cards onto my chocolate mousse—one card proclaiming Richard Radler as president of the Offshore Banking Corporation ("Protect Your Assets with Offshore") and the other introducing Rachael as broker for the Offshore Real Estate Corporation.

I plucked them carefully from the gobs of chocolate and said, "It makes no difference at all to me who sells me my house. But don't I belong to Frieda Sweeten until after dinner?"

"It's a cardinal rule of real estate," said Lisa DaPonto in her first words of the evening, "that the customer doesn't belong to anybody. Don't let any of these people intimidate you, Mr. Field."

She then adjusted the aqua chiffon scarf at her throat in a gesture so arresting and evocative that I recognized at last who she was. Rachael and the general began a private conversation, so I gave my full attention to the police commissioner's wife.

She was dressed tip to toe in aqua, even to an aqua turban, so that the overall effect was that of an oncoming wave. A ravaged beauty, no longer young and somehow pathetic.

"Have you lived here long, Mrs. DaPonto?" I asked.

"Ever since I've been Mrs. DaPonto. That's the past fifteen years. My," she said with a sigh, "it seems so much longer."

"And before that—"

"Oh, from New York—like most everybody else here who isn't from Central America."

"But now you sell real estate in Florida," I said.

She looked at me in astonishment. "Heavens, no. My husband does—on the side, of course. But with half a million people licensed to sell real estate in Florida, the profession— if it can be called that—is somewhat overcrowded."

"What do you do for amusement here?"

"I do what I can for the arts in Fun City."

"Any luck at all?"

"Not much. These people have water on the brain. Sailing, fishing, yachting, swimming. All that moisture causes cell damage, I think. And they like violent sports. Football, mostly. Race cars. Anything they can enjoy vicariously."

"Perhaps all that will change now—now that Antonio Yera has donated Harmonia to the community."

"I don't know," she replied. "It's something like giving a diamond to a child who thinks it's a piece of glass. We'll just have to see."

"Last night was a poor omen, I'll admit."

Mrs. DaPonto's aqua-clad shoulders shivered at the memory.

"Terrible, terrible," she said. "Sherrill Thorne should never have come to Fun City."

"We know that now. It must have seemed a harmless enough idea at the time. Did you know him, by the way?" I slipped in the question nonchalantly.

Lisa DaPonto was a long time answering. She seemed to be toying with her food. In the interval, Sweeten excused himself from the table. Rachael Radler looked up and explained his departure—"Prostate problems!"—and went back to her plate. I waited patiently for Lisa to speak.

"I never met Mr. Thorne before last night," she said at last.

"You were one of the pilgrims at intermission?"

"Pilgrims? Yes, I suppose that was the idea. We sponsors were supposed to pay our respects. That wasn't why I went, though."

"Why did you go?"

"Why do you ask?"

Lisa DaPonto may not have been in real estate, but she certainly had picked up on its First Commandment: Always answer a question with a question.

"That procession into Thorne's box was totally inexplicable. Anyone who knew Thorne would have known better. Forgive me, but I thought you might easily have known him."

"Impossible!" Lisa looked genuinely frightened. "How

could I have known him? I told you! I never met him before last night.''

"Not socially, perhaps. But professionally, I think you knew him very well. He surely knew you.''

"He didn't!'' she wailed. "He didn't remember me at all! I went in there to show him that Lisa Lopez Jacir was alive and living it up in Fun City. And she didn't even have the satisfaction of being recognized!''

Our conversation—up to Lisa's outburst—had been in hushed tones. As luck would have it, Sweeten rejoined us then and latched on to the last name heard.

"Lisa Lopez Jacir!'' he bellowed. "What a singer! Once heard, never forgotten!''

Rachael looked up. "Maybe I should get her for our artists series?''

"Oh do, do,'' said Sweeten, his eyes misting over. "I used to fly up to New York just to hear her. Paid any price I had to for the tickets. Scalpers made a fortune when Lisa Lopez Jacir sang. She was so awful, she was wonderful!

"Where is she now, I wonder?'' asked the general.

Right in front of you, thought I to myself, and mad enough to kill you.

19

QUITE true. Everything the general said was true. What Anna Russell parodies, Lisa Lopez Jacir delivered in all good faith. The scoop up to the wrong note. The exaggerated hand gestures. The change of stance, like a football player digging his toes in the turf, when she climbed for a high C. Never once made it, either.

And through it all, the conspiracy of audiences and critics. That was the really mystical part of it. Lisa Lopez Jacir wanted to be a great singer. The fact that she could not carry a tune didn't at all deter her. She had the money, and she had the time.

Thorne it was who made her fashionable. He caught one of her recitals and wrote a tongue-in-cheek review so hilarious that it is quoted verbatim to this day. After that, her concerts were packed. Nothing appeals more to the quirky sense of humor of New Yorkers than a good joke on somebody else.

But all things pass. With no explanation at all, the yearly recitals evaporated like dew in the night. Most people assumed she had died. Maybe she had simply read—and understood—Thorne's review.

I glanced toward Lisa, in an agony of shame at what I'd begun. She looked awash and drowning in a sea of aqua. Poor Lisa had come a long way—to a place she hated—to seek anonymity. She sought her privacy even at the expense of marrying a buffoon like DaPonto. But no amount of pity could erase the fact that I had found one person with ample motive for murdering Thorne. It was Sweeten, at the moment, who was receiving her murderous stare. Though, of course, he couldn't see that.

Sweeten was launching into a long list of anecdotes about the hapless Jacir. In a last-ditch effort to change the subject, I broke in.

"Mrs. DaPonto and I were just discussing the last moments of Thorne's life."

"Could be a lot worse things," said Sweeten, "than listening to Haydn in your last moments."

"I doubt if he heard much of the Haydn."

"What are you talking about? He wasn't shot until the performance ended."

"By that time, he'd already been strangled. I knew it the moment I saw him."

Sweeten's half-blind eyes bulged.

"Strangled? What possible evidence do you have for that outrageous statement?"

"The evidence of my eyes. More to the point, of his. There was extensive hemorrhaging of the blood vessels of his eyeballs. His face was bloated and red. All sure signs of death by strangulation. Besides that, the body was stone cold, and there was no loss of blood from the bullets that hit him."

General Sweeten digested this in silence.

"That's why Thorne's remarks during intermission," I continued, "take on such importance. Did you overhear anything in his box? I know how good your hearing is."

The old man gazed absently into the garden. I noticed that the other tables had broken up and that guests were beginning to roam about the gazebo. Sweeten seemed distracted. He made a visible effort to collect himself.

"Nothing. I heard absolutely nothing. There were too many people in there all at once, too much talking going on. When do you think he was actually killed?"

"I don't know. It's hard to narrow down the precise moment. I looked up at Thorne during the second movement of the Haydn symphony, and I thought he'd fallen asleep. He

was dead by then. He may have been dead sometime before
I noticed him.''

''I can't believe any of this,'' insisted Sweeten. ''If a murder took place during the performance, someone was sure to
notice.''

''You're wrong. All eyes were glued to that spectacle onstage. The only light was candlelight. All of it onstage. For
the only time that night, the rest of the hall was in darkness,
and our attention was fully diverted. We wouldn't have noticed a murder committed before our eyes, because our eyes
were elsewhere.''

The old general mulled this over in silence. He stared out
blindly toward the grounds where the other patrons had gathered. Then he rose and started to leave.

Rachael, soul of diplomacy, called after him, ''It's a simple operation, General. You really should see a doctor about
all those visits to the john.''

Vance Sweeten paused, after a few steps, and turned half-
way around. He seemed to be talking to Lisa DaPonto, but I
assumed he meant me.

''Can we talk for a few minutes?'' he said.

''Certainly. Why not now?''

''No, not now. At the fountain in half an hour. I may have
some answers for you.''

Then he trundled off toward the cluster of patrons, as Rachael Radler led me down the garden path.

So to speak.

In all fairness, Rachael had no other choice. She had a
drunken husband on her hands and no other able-bodied man
in sight to help her.

Between us, we shoved, propped, and steered Richard
Radler through the gardens—a long walk, let me tell you—
and up the elevator to my room.

Rachael and I laid him out on my bed, where he looked
like a gargoyle lying in state.

''I think Dick's had a tad too much wine,'' said Rachael.
''It's upset his stomach.''

No comment. The aura of whiskey enveloped Radler's
prone form, sending me to open all the windows before as-
phyxia set in.

Rachael watched me. Since I neither condemned nor applauded, she apparently decided that a small confidence was in order.

"I don't admit this to everyone, John," she conceded, "but I'm beginning to think Dick has a Problem."

I thought it was already universally conceded that the banker had a Problem, as the euphemism goes. Still, I went along with the gag.

"How long has he had this . . . this . . ."

"Problem? It's been growing for a long time now, ever since we arrived in Florida. I think it dates back to the time his lip was split."

"Split lip?" I echoed brightly. "Didn't that interfere with his drinking?"

"Not at all. But it wrecked his embouchure."*

"What happened? What wrecked his embouchure?" I bent over Radler's inert form and saw a large scar, still visible on both lips.

Rachael seemed intent on changing the subject.

"Oh, look!" she exclaimed. "You've got a VCR!"

"Richard has an LIP. . . . Was your husband a musician?"

"I wonder if all the rooms have a videocassette recorder? How thoughtful! I'll bet you don't even know how to work it."

She walked over to the television set in the corner and whirled a few knobs and dials.

"There!" she said. "It's all set. Last night's performance is being rebroadcast tonight. I've set it to record it automatically for you."

"Thanks. You were saying—"

"The whole thing's on tape. Even my appearance onstage at intermission. I should have worn blue, damn it!"

"Your husband couldn't have been"—my memory was finally churning up names—"the famous horn virtuoso of the Symphonic Orchestra of Boston, could he?"

"Whatever makes you think that?"

---

* Embouchure: the position and use of the lips in producing a musical tone on a wind instrument. Like a golfer's stance, a musician's embouchure requires years of development.

"The one who dropped out of sight more than twenty years ago? There were rumors galore. I even heard he'd had a fight with a critic. Lots of names surfaced, among them—"

"Sherrill Thorne's. Yes. That bastard . . . It was Sherrill Thorne, all right. Dick was confined in a mental institution for a short period. Not unusual with horn players. All those vibrations going through the head are bound to affect you, after a while. He recovered and played one bad performance. Thorne destroyed him in his review. You can understand why Dick felt compelled to take after Thorne with a knife."

"None of this came out in the papers," I said.

"Thorne never pressed charges. I'll say that much for him. But the SOB dropped him right afterward. No other orchestra would hire him after that incident. So we came down here. To the end of the earth. Tony Yera helped him. I don't know what we would have done without Tony then. But banking isn't Dick's cup of tea. Luckily, I turned out to be a good real estate salesman. That's what's saved us."

Rachael seemed exhausted by her confession. Whatever her shortcomings in other areas, I knew that Rachael Radler was a twentieth-century phenomenon, maybe one of the last of the species: a devoted wife, a woman who would do anything for her husband. I wondered if she would pick up where her husband left off, on revenge.

"Did you know Sherrill Thorne?" My question was blunt.

"Last night was the first time I saw him in twenty years. And I didn't make Dick go in with me to his box. That was simply asking too much."

"Surely you realize," I said, "that you were one of the last people to see and talk to Sherrill Thorne."

"He didn't even know me! I guess he wouldn't—I'm a hundred pounds heavier than I used to be. What are you suggesting? That I lagged behind and killed him?"

I looked at her tired face. A face devoid of guile or cunning. It had a housewife's careworn look of love and devotion and worry. For all life's problems, Rachael would always be there with a little chicken soup.

"I'm not suggesting anything," I said, "except that Richard is a very lucky man. But you are an invaluable witness. I want you to recall everything you saw in Thorne's box from the stage and everything you heard when you went up there."

Rachael sat down on the end of the bed. The headboard rose accordingly.

"I'm not sure I can remember. I'll try. Tony was talking to Thorne while I was announcing the football scores. I had a hard time talking above them. Very rude. They could see me there."

"Then Tony left. I saw the Sweetens sitting in their box, like two old crows. I thought it was odd they didn't introduce themselves when all the other patrons were paying their respects."

"Everybody?"

"They were packed like sardines in there. Come to think of it, I don't think I saw Bob O'Reilly. Miguel Ochelly was actually snoozing on the couch in the anteroom. He was even there when Hedda and I left."

Rachael looked at me shrewdly.

"Really, John, I don't know why you're asking all these questions. Or do I? I did overhear your ridiculous conversation with General Sweeten out at the gazebo."

"You did? Did anyone else hear that?"

"The general booms out everything. And you—whether you know it or not—have a carrying voice."

I looked at my watch. Just five more minutes until my meeting with Vance Sweeten.

"Trust me," I said. "I won't take much more of your time. Now try to remember. What did Thorne say to you and Ms. Hasse?"

"Well, he didn't grab my hand and look deep into my eyes, if that's what you mean."

"He did that with Hedda? That's odd. What did he say?"

"His back was to me. He complimented her and asked her if she was German. Or something like that. With that German name, you expect Hedda to have a thick European accent."

"What was Hedda's reaction?"

"Well, I suppose that's why I remember the incident at all. Her reaction was so surprising. I thought she was about to slap him. Then the lights began to flash, and we left."

"You were the last ones there?"

Rachael considered. "No, Miguel Ochelly was still there. Napping. I jabbed him and told him to go back to his own box. He was groggy, but I'm sure he was picking up to leave when Hedda and I departed.''

She moved from the bed to a small cane-backed chair, straining its fragile, curved legs to unexpected pressure. In front of her, Richard Radler slept on—oblivious to both of us—in my bed.

It was time now to meet Vance Sweeten, and I left the Radlers to each other while I stepped out on the balcony and surveyed the scene in the courtyard. Not a sign of the old general.

Then I saw Hedda Hasse racing toward the doors below. She looked up at me and shouted something.

Surely my ears were playing tricks on me.

I raced down the steps outside my room and met her in the courtyard. She grabbed me by the hand and pulled me in the direction of the gazebo.

''What's the matter? What is it?'' I could make no sense of what she was saying.

''I told you!'' She yelled the words. ''It's the general! You've got to get him out of there!''

''Out of where?''

''The canal! He's fallen in the canal! The crocodiles are loose in there!''

20

I was too late to save General Sweeten. Too late even to save any sign of him, except for the smashed, thick spectacles I found on the bank.

I managed to lure the six reptiles out of the canal and back into their pit. Then I sought out DaPonto, who insisted that the whole thing was an accident. The general had taken a little walk after dinner, he said, and in his sightless stupor had tripped off the bridge spanning the canal. Probably drank too much during the evening. That, coupled with a weak latch on the crocodile pit, had—

You get the picture. I protested that Sweeten had had no more than one glass of wine at dinner. But what could I prove? The bolt that held those crocodiles in their pen could have been opened by anybody. Even perhaps by a determined crocodile. Perhaps. That bolt looked just fine to me, by the way, but I reinforced it with a steel bar, just to be on the safe side.

The police came. And the ambulance. But there was nothing to take away. That was the most horrible aspect of the killing.

All the guests had heard Sweeten's screams and ran to the bridge. There they stood helplessly and watched the carnage. Only Hedda ran for help, if I can be said to be of help. DaPonto must have radioed for rescue units, but they arrived even later than I. There was no one left to rescue. No one suggested the beasts be destroyed. They were, after all, an endangered species. Though not so endangered as an old man who knew too much.

Our virtues become, ultimately, our sins. I had no doubt that General Sweeten knew Thorne's killer, but that his code of honor made him first confront the murderer with his knowledge. That would be playing fair. The General Sweetens of this world live by a code of ethics observed, they believe, by all men. Duty, honor, and country. That's the way it goes. Not a single one of the suspects, unhappily, went to West Point.

Where they did go, while I was with the Radlers, was my pressing concern. I tried to find out, but the guests were a sorry, dispirited lot. Silent. Frightened.

This time, murder had struck closer to home. Quickly. Brutally. They knew it, too. Maybe they were simply confused on everybody's whereabouts. And maybe they just didn't want to think about it too much.

We trailed back from the bridge toward the mansion. Even Dick Radler, shocked out of his stupor, and Rachael, stunned into speechlessness, had joined the scene. Now I saw Rachael Radler and Connie Weber shepherding the distraught widow through the gardens. The Argentos walked with O'Reilly and Lange. Miguel Ochelly had commandeered Hedda and was escorting her back. I followed. Alone. As usual.

When we arrived at the courtyard, I saw Antonio Yera hug Frieda Sweeten. Tears were streaming down his cheeks, tears intermingled with the hysterical sobs of Frieda.

The night had been clear and filled with breezes. Now—suddenly—the heavens opened. A wrenching downpour, so violent we were soaked in seconds. With the rains came winds, galelike blasts that sent us scurrying for cover.

We all rushed inside to Yera's spacious drawing room. There, through the long, arched windows, we watched the storm gain in fury and momentum.

Frieda was taken upstairs, sedated, and put to bed. Hedda and Connie and Rachael stayed with her until a drug-induced sleep conquered the old woman. Even then, Hedda remained.

As the evening wore on, our host ordered food and drink

for his unexpected guests. Later, he offered them beds, too, an offer accepted by all. No one could stir out in that storm.

This was not a rain, this was a monsoon. I would even have called it a hurricane, but everyone assured me that such a thing was not possible at that time of year in Florida.

I am not a fanciful man. Still, this sudden storm. So harsh and unforeseen. It seemed to me that Providence had trapped us there. And that Providence was up to no good.

One by one, people began excusing themselves and going up to bed. When the last guest had departed, I walked upstairs to check on Hedda and her charge. Mrs. Vance Sweeten was sound asleep, tears and mascara staining her withered cheeks. Hedda slept in a large chair beside her. I took a comforter off the bed and placed it on Sleeping Beauty.

Then I left the premises and trudged up to my own room, just in time to catch a phone call from Seamus Connacht.

Full of news and data, he was. Connacht has the breezy air of an Irish spalpeen, but he's a deadly serious scholar. I couldn't have picked a better candidate to scour the morgue of the *New York Globe*. Like all Irishmen, Seamus is a born gossip, with a nose for news.

"You won't believe the facts I've got for you, my lad," said Seamus. "Almost too good to be true."

He then went on to relate everything I'd found out on my own. That Antonio Yera had three wives and one mistress. That they, in turn, had their own succession of alliances. That one wife was named Constanze—I cut him short. I knew all that. That Robert Radler was first horn for the Symphonic Orchestra of Boston until an unfortunate incident—

"Thanks, Seamus," I said, "but I think we have to release Radler from the string of suspects for tonight's murder. He's an excellent candidate, though, for Thorne's."

"Tonight's murder!" shrieked Connacht. Then and there, I knew I had said too much if I expected any further help from Seamus's call. Quickly, I summed all that had happened and then begged off offering any speculation.

"You're destroyed thinkin', John. It's time you got some sleep. Lock your door, for God's sake, and get out of there tomorrow. It's not your problem."

I acquiesced. To all but the last. It was my problem when I might have prevented Sweeten's death.

"Oh, one more thing," said Seamus. "Have you got any access to *Globe* microfilms down there?"

"I suppose so. Yes, I do. The town library is here at Harmonia. Why?"

"There's a picture that might interest you." Connacht gave me the date, the page, and the column.

"Write it down, John," he said. "Have you got a pen there?"

I did. He then told me what I could do with it.

Seamus called me around midnight.

The next time I looked at my watch, it was 1:00 A.M. What happened in that hour, I really can't tell you—except to say that these episodes occur from time to time with me. When my conscious mind can't solve problems, my subconscious takes over and does the job.

When I returned to the land of the living, I found myself seated on the bed. Spread out before me were: the scraps of Thorne's program, an inscribed cuff link, a torn ticket stub, the manuscript of the Yera Concerto. Late as it was, I felt this sudden urge to call James Goldman in Mexico City. Though 1:00 A.M.. here, it was only 10:00 P.M. in Mexico City. Goldy would be coming back from his recital any minute now.

Allowing time for encores, I decided to give Goldy a few minutes' grace. Meanwhile, I rummaged around for a phone directory. At the back of my night table drawer, I found one so old that area codes weren't even listed. Filled with musical doodling it was, but I kept it on my knee while I talked with the operator. Eventually, she put me through to the violinist.

"Congratulations, Goldy!" I said, with vim and enthusiasm.

"John, isn't it? Thank you. I was brilliant tonight."

"You always are."

"One tries. The audience seemed pleased, you know. They demanded five encores."

"Were you prepared?"

"I was prepared to play seven. One never knows."

"They love you in Mexico City, don't they, Goldy?"

"They love me everyplace. They *appreciate* me in Mexico City, much as Prague appreciated Mozart."

One had to admire the way James Goldman identified with the greatest mind of music. No shame at all.

"Helps a lot," I continued, "that you speak Spanish. You do, don't you?"

"I get by. Why? I thought this was a call of congratulation. Why do I smell a rat?"

"Let's just say it's a double-edged call—to praise, on one hand, and to beg, on the other. Do you think you could track down in the local archives a concert held there on—" I gave him a date and continued. "Find out who performed what. Is that too much trouble?"

He seemed to think so. I waited for the rumblings to subside, then added, "And while you're at it, I need you to check the public records—" This time the rumblings erupted into a volcano. I had to repeat my request of what I wanted him to search the public records *for* and to temper my demand with a touch of blackmail.

"You wouldn't want to return to Fun City as a material witness, would you, Goldy? What if your violin string turns up in Thorne's box? As I suspect it will any minute now. The closer I get to the murderer, the more evidence will pop up against the musicians. You, most of all, since the murder weapon was a violin string."

Goldman saw the reasonableness of my request, after a little contemplation. He promised to call me the next day.

After that, I locked up my small pile of clues, undressed, and went to bed.

But not for long.

Lightning struck the South Tower, not too far from where I was sleeping. The sound of shattering glass mixed with the peal of rolling thunder. But that was outside. Inside, near my door, I could hear an awful commotion.

Between human and divine force, I opted for human and decided to check the hallway. All power was out, so in the darkness, I fell across the night table, stubbed my toe on the bedpost, fumbled at the door bolt, and—all in all—wasted far too much time wending my way through the blackness.

In the distance, I heard the sound of footsteps echoing up

through the stairwell. Maybe I could take the elevator—but no, that would be inoperable now.

I dashed for the stairwell. And stepped on something soft. A body. Very much alive.

"John! I can't get up! Help me!" Whispered words. Frightened.

It was Hedda Hasse. Sleepwalking again.

Small wonder she couldn't get up. The idea was that she never get up at all.

I pulled the knife that was pinning her dark mantle of hair to the floor. It had grazed her scalp. No harm done.

I gathered her up, trembling and shaken, and took her into my room.

21

THIS is not one of those books that tells all. There are, after all, limits.

Some hours later, from the depths of a down pillow, Hedda was remarking that she "didn't feel good at all."

I assured her that she felt wonderful. Simply wonderful. Then I considered her statement.

"You mean that you don't feel well?"

"John, do you have to insist on points of grammar? Even in your sleep?"

"That was not my sleep," I said huffily. "There is a fine distinction at issue here. To say you don't feel good implies I have failed you somehow. To say you don't feel well suggests medical assistance is needed. Which is it?"

"I feel good, but I don't feel well."

"Ah," I said, turning over and smiling broadly, "then I am indeed in a position to make you feel better."

She raised herself up on an elbow and stared out the rain-pelted windows.

"I feel a draft—a terrible draft. Don't you notice it?"

"No," I said blissfully. "It's probably the air-conditioning. Maybe the power's back on."

"I have an awful headache, besides."

"You're just remembering your narrow escape out in the

hall. Put it out of your mind. Nothing's going to happen to you now.''

"Are you sure the door is still locked?''

"Positive. And I still have the only set of keys. No one can get in here. I'll find you some aspirin, though. They'll even help you sleep.

"Counting up your number of close shaves since first we met,'' I continued, "you should be subject to continual tension headaches. How did you get that broken foot, by the way?''

"John,'' she said, in some irritation, "stop sleuthing. Just get the aspirin.''

I did as I was bidden. Gave her the aspirin. Climbed back into bed. Helped her feel better.

It was some time later—an hour or so—when I too began to feel a draft. Hedda was sound asleep by then, so I got up as noiselessly as possible and began to investigate.

I traced the cold to a chink of limestone that had come loose near the top of the door to the balcony. To the left, in the corner of the room.

Wind damage. Or could it be—lightning damage?

I stepped out through the door onto the balcony. The wind was still blowing at gale force, and the rains were heavier than ever. It was not the best of all possible worlds out there.

Peering down from the rail of the balcony, I could dimly see where the force of the lightning bolt had struck. In the courtyard. It had shattered the fountain. The hideous sculpture was smashed into a crumbling heap. Could that have been the sound of shattering glass I'd heard?

Apparently, the lightning bolt had not hit the South Tower, as I'd thought, but the charge had come close enough to cause a power outage—probably for the entire mansion. There was no light to be seen anywhere.

I crossed the balcony landing to Thorne's door. Like mine, the long, glass-paneled door was unharmed, protected apparently by the eaves of the roof. I tried the door. Unlocked.

A wiser man would have turned around and climbed back into bed. But I was curious. I turned the handle and entered Thorne's bedroom.

* * *

A half-hour later, I was back on the balcony again. Now dawn was breaking through the rain. Just enough light to make me realize that I had not been wrong about that sound of glass.

I leaned over and picked up several small pieces of stained glass. Then I looked up to see where they had come from.

Above me was the exact counterpart of the window in the North Tower—a small rose window, embellished with a four-bar grille and located directly between Thorne's room and mine. Why hadn't I noticed it before?

The grille was still intact, but the window itself was in shards. Yet the wind must have been of tornado strength to smash a window protected by four iron bars.

An odd wind, one might say, to strike a recessed rose window. And yet to leave two full-length glass doors untouched.

Where did that window go? It wasn't in my room, and it wasn't in Thorne's.

I lunged upward, grabbed onto the iron grille, and pulled myself up to look through the window that went noplace.

22

SOMETIME during the early morning hours, power was restored at Harmonia. For how long, one could not say. The storm seemed violent as ever to me.

When Hedda awoke at around 9:00 A.M., she found me watching the taped recording of Sunday's performance.

"What are you doing?" she asked.

"Watching a murder. Care to pull up a chair?"

"Why have you tuned out the sound?"

"Only one sound matters. I'll turn it up when that moment comes."

We watched in silence for the next ninety minutes.

I told her nothing of what I'd found outside.

"What do we do now?" asked the singer.

"First of all, we get you some protection, while I get some proof. You're not to be left alone for a minute in this place. Right now, help me find the damn keyring the security guard lent me. Do you trust him, by the way?"

"Luis Rodriguez? I do. As a matter of fact, I have good reason to trust him."

"What reason?"

"It's a long story. Let's find the keys."

Hedda found them, as a matter of fact. Under the false bottom of the armoire. In a most logical place, just as I had predicted. I removed the key to my bedroom from the ring, then replaced the keyring in its hiding place.

We locked up the room and took a maze of back corridors to the small office of the security guard. With stern instructions to guard her carefully and to take her to the kitchen for some lunch, I left Hedda and made arrangements to meet them later.

"That gun is loaded, Luis?"

"Habsolutely, Meester Feeld."

"You'll use it if you have to?"

"Weeth great pleasure."

"What are you going to do now, John?" asked Hedda.

"I'm going to spread the word among our friends that there'll be old movies at the Hall of Mirrors tonight."

"Will you tell them that you know the murderer?"

"No—I'll let that be my little surprise."

I kissed her lightly on the top of the head and started for the door.

Before closing it after me, I said, "Why didn't you tell me the truth about why you came down here?"

She blew a kiss at me.

"I'll let that be *my* little surprise."

I had no sooner returned to my room than the phone rang. It was James Goldman. Positively jubilant.

"There are times, John, when you are prescient. You were absolutely right. Whatever made you think of that possibility?"

"Something Thorne said. And I should have thought of it long before. I might have prevented one death." And I told him all about General Sweeten's cruel end.

Eric Hanson taught at the State University of New York at Albany when he wasn't concertizing. So he was admirably placed to do me a favor.

I called and asked for two.

He guessed, he said, he owed me that.

I couldn't, I said, agree more.

"No, John, I can't send agents over in a helicopter in this kind of weather."

"You must," I said. "I can't keep a murderer penned up here once the sun shines again. There was almost another killing last night, and tonight is even more likely—"

Bill McIntire was an old friend of mine long before he became Special Agent in Charge of the FBI Field Office in Fun City. Barring a certain negativism in his makeup—he tells you all the reasons he can't do something while solving the means whereby he can—he is a splendid law enforcer.

"Their ferries aren't even running," he said morosely.

"Surely you can requisition a battleship."

We argued on and on.

"Mr. Field," cautioned the librarian, "you can't take these out of here. Those are reference materials."

"But these are—"

"Reference materials," she repeated.

Now and then, a man must acknowledge defeat. Have you ever seen a bear guarding her cubs? A librarian defending her books is far more formidable. Naturally, I capitulated.

Just as well. She went to her magic machine—a Xerox of sorts, that could copy, enlarge, count, and—if asked—do tumbling tricks. Ah, the wonders of technology.

I left victorious.

23

TIME was running out. I had only thirty minutes before meeting Hedda and Rodriguez at the Hall of Mirrors. We had a lot to do after that. In the meantime, it was up to me to spread the word to the patrons, "Let us entertain you" being its theme.

I dropped into the dining room, where all but the composer and Frieda were lunching away.

"Looks like we're going to have nothing better to do," said Rachael, her tact still intact. "This is the worst storm I've seen in years."

"Movies, you say," commented DaPonto, picking his teeth. "From the library, I suppose?"

"Make it a scary one, John," said Lisa. "Nothing cerebral tonight."

"That's a three-syllable word, my dear. Aren't you exceeding yourself?" A few more comments like that, I thought, and DaPonto would find arsenic in his soup. I'd put it there myself, as a favor to Lisa.

I had no appetite to join them, nor did they press me to do so. So I turned on my heel and braved, as they say, the elements.

The rains were coming down so hard that I skirted the courtyard entirely and walked through the encircling sheltered arcade. Right past Antonio Yera's wing.

He saw me and invited me into his lair.

And quite a lair it was. Roughly the size of southern France, barring the Riviera. We moved into the same drawing room all of us had occupied last night—after the killing. I had been too disoriented then to notice my surroundings, but today the opulence of the setting overpowered me.

Ornate wood paneling, flecked with gold-leaf trim, accented hand-painted silk panels extending from floor to ceiling. White marble floors stretched the entire expanse of the wing—from the courtyard gallery to the sculptured terrace facing the sea. An airiness dominated the huge room, a perfect blending of captured sunlight and man-made luxury. Florida beauty without Florida heat. The pleasure without the pain.

I told him that I had planned a little entertainment for the evening in the Hall of Mirrors. Old movies, I said. Something to relieve the boredom. Did he mind? I would enliven the evening with my own commentaries, since I am something of a film buff myself.

Yera acquiesced with a nod of his head. His mind was elsewhere.

"Have you got the manuscript?" he asked, getting right to the point.

"Not at the moment. I stopped by earlier," I lied, "but—"

"Perfectly all right. Sometime before you leave, though. When *are* you leaving?"

I paused just long enough before answering to indicate that the question was a rude one.

"I'm scheduled to play in Paris tomorrow night. Naturally, I'm as anxious to leave as—" I let the sentence dangle in the air, implications intact.

"My dear fellow! You know you are most welcome at Harmonia—a musician of your stature! You couldn't get out now anyway. I understand the airport is still closed because of the storm."

I appeared to be mollified.

"I'll be performing the Yera Concerto in London this fall—" I began.

Yera pricked up his ears like a basset hound who's just

spotted a rabbit. I made a mental note to suggest some such change in program to my management.

"—and I don't think they've selected the contralto yet. I'm tempted to recommend Ms. Hasse, after her performance on Sunday, but she's virtually unknown in the musical world. Can you tell me something about her?"

"You've heard her sing. What do you want to know?"

"Where's she from? What are her background and musical credentials?"

"I'm sure Hedda would tell you if you asked her, but I'll tell you all I know. Born in Frankfurt, I believe, and raised by an uncle. She was a full scholarship student at Juilliard for four years, where she attracted a lot of attention in student performances. As you know, though, New York City is not the place for a singer to start. It's the place they aspire to and—eventually—win."

"But Hedda is not an ordinary singer, is she?"

"Hedda," agreed Yera, "is a remarkable talent."

"Why did she come here? Why not Europe, where most young singers get their start?"

"Really, Mr. Field, I couldn't answer for Hedda. You must ask her that. Can I offer you some sherry?"

I accepted the offer, and while he rang for a servant, I walked toward three life-size portraits that hung in an alcove—rather like a small shrine in a large cathedral, when you think about it.

"Your wives?" I asked. He wasn't the only one who could get right to the point.

A dark, young page brought our sherry and retreated into the wings. Yera then answered my question.

"I was greatly honored," he said, "to be loved by three beautiful and talented women."

We did the tour, the composer providing the commentary.

"This is my first wife—the famous Mary Calnan."

I looked at the portrait in question and into the soft eyes of the Irish singer. She had the typical Celtic coloring—red hair and green eyes—and the imperious expression of the prima donna. Pure accident, surely, that she was posed to stare, in apparent anger, straight into the eyes of her successor.

"Did you ever hear Mary Calnan sing, Mr. Field?"

"No—only through recordings. Never in person."

"Pity you never saw her. She was far more than a singer. She was an actress who lent credibility to every word. Mary was only thirty-six when this was painted—it was right after she lost almost two hundred pounds."

"Her voice was never the same after that, was it?"

"Unhappily, no. She lost the weight for me, you know, to make herself more attractive in my eyes. The fact is, though, she never learned to produce her tone correctly—relaxed, from deep within the diaphragm. Once the weight was gone— the only thing that sustained her—the voice was gone, too. Pity."

We passed on to the next in line, Regina Dulcino.

"A distinctive face, don't you think, Mr. Field?"

Distinctive, I thought, and immensely self-satisfied. Dark complexion punctuated by shrewd, dark eyes. Black hair, dramatically pulled away from aquiline features.

"She had the Italian temperament," said Yera. "Generous, passionate, and fiery. Tragic that she was robbed of her ultimate triumph. She would have been the toast of the Met."

"Perhaps," I said. Certainly New York would have been fascinated by Regina, I thought, but never charmed.

The third painting was unrecognizable to me. Pressed, I would have said Goldilocks, judging from the strawberry-blond curls that framed a vapid, chalk-white face. A flapper face, if such a thing exists, distinguished only by a nose too large. The face was smiling its head off.

"Don't you recognize Constanze Weber?" asked Yera. "She's older now, of course, but that smile—that's her real badge of beauty."

"She has—changed, somehow. Maybe she doesn't smile so much anymore. Or maybe I've never seen her smile."

"Nobody in real estate smiles much nowadays. We've overbuilt down here, you know."

I looked all around the alcove and, finally, came out with it.

"Isn't someone missing here?"

"Yes—but so far, I haven't been able to persuade Hedda to pose for her portrait."

"No, not Hedda. Sherrill Thorne mentioned your *affaire de coeur* with the great Theresa von Trattner."

"Did he indeed?" Yera's manner was cold in the extreme. "I really did my best to dissuade him of it."

"There was no truth to it at all?"

"It was a brief, wild infatuation. I left Connie for her—for a time—but Connie was good enough to take me back when I came to my senses."

"I know so little about Theresa von Trattner. What was she like?"

" 'She had a heart'—how shall I say"—Yera groped for the words—" 'too soon made glad, too easily impressed.' "

"You mean—there were others?"

" 'She liked all she looked upon,' " said Yera, " 'and her looks went everywhere.' "

"You have no picture—no likeness—of her at all?"

"None. Why should I?"

"No reason. It's just that I've always wondered what she looked like. None of her albums contain a photograph."

"That's because she was camera shy," said Yera. "She was a woman without vanity. Strange, you know, for she was immensely beautiful. Blond hair, a complexion smooth as porcelain—"

"Blue eyes, I imagine."

Yera cast his own brown eyes into my hazel orbs and said, "I honestly don't remember. What was most remarkable about her features was that everyone described them differently. To this day, I can't think what she looked like."

"Sherrill Thorne would have been interested in these reminiscences, you know. What a loss it is for you that such an influential critic will not write your biography."

Antonio Yera sat down on a white brocade love seat and sipped on his sherry.

"A terrible loss," he admitted. "In the long run, though, perhaps it's a good thing."

"How do you mean?"

"Thorne was getting hung up—surely you know this—on what he perceived as romantic allusions in my music. Love letters to Hedda, he called them. And, of course, she has been a great inspiration to me."

"But the allusions are there," I said. "They abound in the music. Thorne was quite right about the Hedda motifs."

"My dear Mr. Field," said Yera coldly, "there are only

seven notes in the scale—plus their respective sharps and flats.
It is inevitable that I would repeat some motifs, especially
since I like to work with short themes. So did Beethoven. I
wonder what Sherrill Thorne would have made out of the so-
called victory motif—the ta-ta-ta-*tum*—of the Fifth Symphony. Something to do with his love life?''

"I wouldn't put it past him. Or past Beethoven, either."

"Thorne kept asking me what the themes and motifs
meant." The composer was warming to his subject. "And I
kept telling him that he was asking the wrong question. All
that counted was what I was able to do with the themes, how
I could release their musical meaning."

"But composers do drop biographical clues in their music.
Robert Schumann did it all the time."*

"Perhaps," conceded Yera. Partially. "And perhaps he
wrote the composition first and added the title and explanation later. There is much evidence to support this now re-
garding the Abegg Variations."†

"Then Thorne was wrong," I conceded. Wholly. "After
all, he was a critic, not a composer. But when all is said and
done, he would have been your most sympathetic biographer.
He'd have laid to rest, for example, any doubts about your
political sympathies."

"How do you mean?"

"Thorne never even mentioned to me that you were the
son of Trujillo Yera."

"He knew that. Everybody knows that. Why would I deny
my father? What kind of man would do that? As for my political sympathies—I don't have any. A musician has to stand
above all that foolishness."

There seemed no reply adequate to that statement. I looked
out the windows for some sign of break in the storm. Yera
followed my glance.

---

* Just one example: Schumann (1810–56) based one piece in the piano
cycle "Carnaval" on the word *Asch* (A, E flat—*Es* in German musical
notation—C, and B—or H in German nomenclature). Asch was the
hometown of Schumann's then fiancée.
† Yera was absolutely right about this. Musicologists now insist that
there was no Countess Abegg, the person to whom this piano work was
dedicated and on whose name the variations were based. Schumann
invented her, after completing the composition.

"This weather is spoiling your house hunting, I'm afraid. As soon as it clears, Hedda can take you around, though. I believe Connie has just the house picked out for you."

He must have caught my questioning look, for he amplified.

"You mustn't think that because we're divorced we're not good friends. During my—hiatus, shall we say—from our marriage, Connie became a liberated woman. Marriage can seldom bear two successful people, you know. She's as wrapped up in her work as I am in mine. And she does have the best listings in Fun City."

"Where would you suggest I buy?"

"There's only one place to buy here. That's on Key Cohen. Up until last night, it was completely owned by our little ruling junta. But I think Frieda Sweeten will be wanting to sell soon. Connie mentioned that as a possible home for you."

Now I knew how realtors got their listings in Fun City. They simply consulted the obituary notices. Connie Weber was even quicker off the mark than that.

I checked my watch and saw that I was already ten minutes late for our rendezvous at the Hall of Mirrors.

24

THERE was quite a crowd waiting for me at the Hall of Mirrors—in addition to Hedda and Luis Rodriguez. I made introductions all around before returning the keys of Harmonia to the relieved security guard. One key, of course, was still missing. By that time, though, I'd figured out where it must be and told them so.

Then we entered the auditorium and set to work on the evening's entertainment.

Outside, the rains came down.

Promptly at 8:00 P.M., the crowd assembled. And a sorry, rain-soaked lot they were. Lorenzo DaPonto, cigar in hand, was first to walk down the aisle, trailed at fifteen paces by Lisa. The commissioner looked in vain for an ashtray, then ground out the glowing Havana in the marble floor before seating himself in the front row. He saved a seat for his wife, but I saw her instead take a seat in the third row.

Next, Robert O'Reilly sauntered in, balancing a martini, with Joseph Lange in close attendance. They settled in chairs directly behind Lorenzo DaPonto.

An arthritic Frieda Sweeten hobbled forward, looked with stern disapproval at the stage, the drawn curtain, the harsh lighting, and every one of the patrons. Pointedly, she sat alone—far from the others present—at the extreme end of the second row.

Miguel Ochelly, swaggering far less than usual, walked in next. He seated himself toward the rear of the Hall, for all the world as if he were keeping an eye on everyone there.

The Argentos appeared, still with that air of expecting "Hail to the Chief" (or its Salvaniguan equivalent) to be struck up immediately. They sat close to the police commissioner.

A sober Richard Radler came forward, flanked by two guardians. These were Rachael Radler and Connie Weber, the two chatting happily of this and that. Connie didn't appear to notice Ochelly. The three moved into the center of the second row.

Hedda Hasse shepherded Antonio Yera into the rapidly filling front row, Yera beaming his infatuation, his obsession, his foolishness into the surrounding air. Hedda's expression was inscrutable. If she knew I was watching her, she gave no indication of it.

But then, I was watching them all from the wings of the small stage. I waited for the crowd to get comfortable. Then, when conversation ebbed, I popped out and took command of the situation.

"Thank you for coming tonight, all of you," I began. "In the absence of printed programs, I should tell you that the title of tonight's lecture—"

A moan went up from all assembled there.

"—is 'Crime Deduction and its Relationship to the Metric Patterns of Franz Joseph Haydn'—"

"You said movies!"

"Lecture! My God!"

"—or 'Murder in Three-Quarter Time.' Naturally," I added hastily, "there will be movies. I promise you that!"

Sometimes one has to throw these sops to the crowd, especially a mob intent—as this one seemed to be—on mutiny. When a crowd begins to leave *before* you've begun, I've always noticed, you're really in trouble.

So I drew back the stage curtains—partially—to reveal a large screen. Slightly mollified, the patrons returned. And I continued.

"I thought the best pastime on this dark and stormy night would be to watch a murder and then to watch me solve it.

"As I said before, I appreciate your presence here. It is not easy to visit the scene of violent death and be unmoved. Men still weep at Normandy—more than forty years after the invasion—and some are moved to tears at a book repository in Dallas where a President was shot."

I looked out on that dry-eyed audience and went on.

"These may seem odd parallels to you, these cataclysmic deeds. Yet what happened here Sunday night was just as profound, as earthshaking to the history of music as were those events to the world at large."

"The death of that fat, old critic—is that what you're talking about?" The fat, middle-aged impresario, Rachael Radler, was the first to cast stones.

"The murder of Sherrill Thorne," I continued, "was in fact monstrous. But the need for that murder, plus the recklessness of the means, plus the scale of the deception he unearthed—all these will rock the world of music to its roots.

"If Sherrill Thorne had lived out his life span normally, he would have passed into that nameless oblivion where music critics go when they die. As it was, he stumbled quite accidentally upon a fraud of massive proportions. And he gave his life for that discovery. All things considered, I think he would be delighted by his role in setting the record straight."

"What did he do here that was so remarkable—besides getting himself killed?" Robert O'Reilly was now heard as the voice of compassion.

"In point of fact," I replied, "he lived much longer than the murderer planned. Just long enough to gather the clues needed to piece this puzzle together."

This time there was no heckling from the audience. "But I promised you movies," I said abruptly, "and movies you shall have. What better amusement for a rainy night than to watch a murder committed before your very eyes?"

Above me in the balcony of the Hall of Mirrors, out of the audience's line of vision but not out of mine, stood a group of somberly dressed and somber men. One nodded to me, and I continued.

"We will not watch the entire performance tonight. What we will view are the means, motive, and opportunity for Sherrill Thorne's murder."

The hall lights dimmed, and I began the tape at the point where our ensemble of eight came out on the stage and bowed.

"We'll jump ahead," I said, jiggling the necessary knobs and buttons, "almost to the end of our performance—to that point in time when the music falls off my piano."

The frames raced by in a blur of faces and motions, then

froze on that moment when I wanted the earth to open up and swallow me.

"There, ladies and gentlemen, you see a crisis in the making. The film catches the full panorama of stage action—me, horror-stricken; the page-turner, horror-stricken but fascinated; the pages of music falling down like snowflakes in a blizzard; the door behind me closing shut."

"Now I'll go back a few frames and slow the action," I continued. "This time, with the music stilled to silence and the musicians' fingerwork reduced to invisible taffypulls, try to focus your interest on a new drama taking place in the wings. Watch very carefully here, please—" and I rerolled the tape, silently and in slow motion. "Do you see how a shadow falls across my score?"

They could hardly miss it. Like a shade of doom, the elongated silhouette of a figure cast its image across the stage and across the manuscript on the piano.

"I'll turn up the volume slightly here. If you listen carefully, you'll notice background sounds above the music. There now! Listen! Someone rousting around backstage. The sound of a falling object. A violin case, from which the murderer steals a D string. The means of the murder—

"Now see what happens!"

For all to see, the stage door behind me swung shut. The laws of physics being what they are, the closing door created a breeze that wrought its magic on the music and me. Like a flight of pigeons, the pages wafted high in the air. Like a homing missile, I dove after them.

"Now for the sound—" and I turned up the volume.

Above the soft passages of the music, Sherrill Thorne's voice could be heard shouting "Careless!" The camera was trained on the stage, not on the boxes, revealing no trace of emotion on my face nor any of the performers'.

"Meester Field, I felt so sorry for you then," said the voice belonging to Luscious Alicia. "Such a rude thing to say—just because the pages fell down."

"Unthinkable," I replied, "when Sherrill Thorne could clearly see what had happened, though we could not. We were in the grip of panic because the performance threatened to break apart.

"Panic often occurs during a performance. The unplanned occurs time and time again. I've had keys fly off the piano. I've seen a cello slide right down to a slippery floor, a violinist break a string during a solo passage, a soprano lose her top notes, a ballerina take a pratfall.

"But any critic knows that what is crucial is not the crisis itself but how the performer deals with it. Savoir-faire counts—nothing else. That's part of what makes a live performance so exciting—the hairbreadth quality of it—the 'how is he going to get out of this one?' syndrome, I call it. Here we are giving the performance of our lives—there I am rescuing pages from the air like it was all part of the act, and there is the music coming out seamless and unstrained.

"Do you really think," I asked, "that Thorne would break with the habits of a lifetime and deliberately wreck the enchantment of those quiet passages?"

"But he did!" yelled Rachael Radler. "That's exactly what he did!"

"Are you sure? Let's put the tape ahead and see."

Our images flashed by to the point where all of our ensemble were standing to the applause. Now the film presented a panoramic view of the stage, the auditorium, and the flanking balcony boxes. Above the clapping, Thorne's roars could be heard: "Hooray! . . . Careless! . . . More!"

"Well, there you have it," I said, freezing the tape. "Thorne shouting out for all the world to hear the motive for his own murder. He will be dead within the hour, and he's already telling us why."

A dead silence fell on the house. My listeners seemed to be waiting for enlightenment.

"Don't you see?" I asked impatiently. "Look at the film: Thorne is standing in his box, but he isn't even facing the stage. You can see his profile very clearly. He's calling out to the box directly opposite."

"That's Tony's box," said Joseph Lange. "Why would he be shouting to Tony?"

"Why indeed?" I signaled toward the balcony, and a form receded in the distance. "Why would he be facing the composer Antonio Saul Yera and calling out another name? For that was what Thorne was doing—crying out a name, the name of the man he recognized, a name he had been trying to dredge out of the past for several minutes.

I added the clincher. "Ever since he first said 'Carlos' in the stillness of a great performance."

25

T HE man in the gray flannel suit walked quietly into the Hall of Mirrors and took a seat directly behind "Antonio Saul Yera." No one seemed to notice his presence until he tapped Yera on the shoulder, whispered in his ear, and ushered the composer from the auditorium.

Our small group watched their departure in shocked silence. Then the clamor began.

"Did you see that?" asked the normally sodden Richard Radler. "They've taken Tony away! They've arrested him just like that!"

"Are you trying to tell us," rasped Frieda Sweeten, "that Tony Yera is somebody named Carlos?"

I turned to the general's widow and said gently, "Somebody named Jorge Carlos Mayor, Mrs. Sweeten. Your husband mentioned the name last night.* Thorne had brought it up even earlier—on the plane—but I was too distracted to realize that he had recalled a name and was continuing our conversation on the plane.

"Then, during the course of the Yera Concerto, Sherrill recognized the identity of the man in the opposite box. He

---

* General Sweeten anglicized the name—you'll recall his obsession about Spanish—but anyone with ears to hear could have picked up that clue.

called out 'Carlos.' In his clipped British accent, it sounded like 'careless'—but the rest of the name escaped him. On the plane, he'd remembered the other two names—Jorge—which sounded like 'hooray' to me—and Mayor—which I misinterpreted as 'more.'

"During the performance, he had involuntarily called out the one name he'd failed to remember on the plane. Later, when we were accepting applause, he called out the entire name—Jorge Carlos Mayor—a name well-known in the annals of music as an operatic tenor of some renown. Not just a tenor but *the* tenor once married to Theresa von Trattner, Yera's mistress. The tenor who had murdered his former wife, then killed himself—according to the news accounts of the time.

"Remember that Thorne had never met Antonio Saul Yera. They had merely corresponded. Instead of Yera, he saw a tenor he knew as gifted, profligate, and dead. Dead owing him money, at that. And while Sherrill Thorne had an old man's failing memory for names, he still had the eyes and ears of a hawk. When you've watched a singer's stance and bearing and mannerisms for years, you're not easily fooled by a name.

"I doubt if Sherrill Thorne knew then the danger he was in. True, he had shouted out the name of an impostor. Out of shock, probably. But I wonder if he didn't suspect—"

Connie Weber took the floor away from me.

"This is ridiculous! Stupid and ridiculous! Don't you think I'd know an impostor? Don't you think I'd know my own husband!"

"Well, I would hope so, Ms. Weber," I said. "But how much do we know about you? How much does anybody know about anybody in a transient community like Fun City? If Jorge Carlos Mayor could carry off a deception for twenty years, why not you? Weren't you just imported for the task—imported to play the role of Yera's ex-wife?"

She stared long and hard at me. Finally, she commented, "I'm not sayin' one more thing until ah see a lawyer."

Connie Weber—or whoever she was—ensconced herself in her chair, where not another word was heard from her.

"Let's get on with the murder, shall we?" I suggested. "So far we've witnessed the means and the motive for

Thorne's murder. The opportunity still eludes us. We'll pick up the tape just before the end of intermission.''

Now the camera focused in on ''Antonio Saul Yera'' talking to Hedda and me. An excellent shot of me, by the way, though the effect was somewhat dissipated by the image of self-swatting repeatedly at head.

''You'll notice,'' I said, as the tape continued to run, ''that the small objects pelting me—spitballs, they seem to be—are coming from the direction of Thorne's box. That would account for the shredded program I found in Thorne's box. This from a man who saved programs religiously, as a buttress to his memory. Now watch what our impostor does.''

As the chandeliers began to dim, Yera/Mayor was caught in the act of both dropping and picking up a handkerchief at his feet.

''Notice that 'Yera' missed seeing what Thorne belted me with in those final seconds of light. It's this''—and I held up a small object—''an ivory cuff link inscribed with a sharp sign.''

''Why?'' asked a voice from the audience. I couldn't identify it.

''Because he was desperate. By that time, he must have known he was trapped in that box and that he would never leave it. He threw the only clue he could give me. An object with a sharp sign on it. Think about that. Stretch your imagination and think about another way of looking at a sharp sign. How is it made? Could it be, for example, a set of initials?''

No one answered. Unimaginative clods. So I dropped that line of reasoning, for the present.

I stopped the tape abruptly and viewed the audience.

''From this point on, I will play the murderer. But I'll need an accomplice. Will you assist me, Ms. Hasse? As we rehearsed earlier today? With just that same split-second timing that you do so well?''

She nodded her assent and walked up the open steps to the stage. At a signal from me, the gold curtains opened fully now to reveal a stage setting—rudimentary but recognizable. The hastily built scaffolding represented the balcony of the Hall of Mirrors, with Thorne's box, the hallway landing, the staircase to the vestibule and patron's terrace—all apparent to the audience. Smaller replicas of the Hall's doors served to duplicate the three doors of the vestibule (stage door, terrace door, auditorium door) and the door to Thorne's box. There was even a makeshift window at the end of the hallway, and this was covered by a sheet, in lieu of floor-length draperies.

I pushed the screen to a point directly beneath the improvised balcony. Then I climbed the steps and headed for the sheet-covered hallway window, while Hedda stood at the stage side of the vestibule's stage door. The tape was running, with sound subdued, while a spotlight traced my movements. I slipped behind the sheet.

On the screen, the lights in the Hall of Mirrors could be seen dimming into blackness. From behind the drawn curtain, the sounds of musicians tuning up were dimly heard. I resumed my running commentary.

"There was no spotlight here Sunday night," I said—emerging from my hiding place—"but here was where a spotlight should have been when all our eyes were glued upon a curtain that was so very slow to open."

"The last visitor has left Thorne's box. I now lock Thorne in and place the key above the doorsill. Yes, I can just manage to reach this smaller door replica. Then I duck behind the gold draperies and wait for all sounds to die. That will mean to me that the Hall of Mirrors is in darkness and the audience is waiting.

"I unlock the door, enter the box, quickly strangle Thorne with the violin string I have stolen backstage."

"Listen for the cough!" Sure enough, in perfect synchronization with the tape, a cough was heard. Only one.

"That cough—the first—was the sign the murder had occurred. One cough inspires another among audiences. They're contagious. Now it's a chorus! Excellent camouflage, of course, for the murderer."

The carpenters had contrived a stuffed dummy for me. I rearranged it into a sleeping position, with head bent down.

"Now I flash a lighter—a signal to someone below me that the murder is completed. But look at the screen. It looks like a battalion of lights. It is only one—reflected over and over by the angled mirrors.

"Many actions occur simultaneously now," I continued, "for my accomplice is responding to my signal." Another spotlight focused on Hedda, poised at the entrance to the vestibule from the stage door.

"My cohort slips through the stage door and unlocks the terrace door for the Marielito, who runs up the steps, not noticing that the door has been deadbolted behind him and that he, like Thorne, is now trapped in the Hall of Mirrors. My accomplice is now free to return to the hall. Just sixty-two seconds have passed, and no one could have noticed anyone's absence or return in the total darkness."

Hedda left the stage, and the spotlight once more focused on myself alone. On the screen, the tableau of the Haydn setting greeted the eye again. I resumed my role as murderer.

"Upstairs, I lock Thorne's box and replace the key above the sill. I rush along to the head of the steps to meet the hit man. Then something unexpected occurs. I bump into General Vance Sweeten returning—as he did so often—from the men's room. Luckily, he's too blind to recognize me, and I do not speak to him. He stumbles on into his box, and I am there to meet the Marielito when he reaches the top of the steps."

Against the background of the Haydn strains, I enacted the furtive actions of the killer.

"I show the Marielito where the key is hidden. Then I hide him behind the draperies, with instructions that he is to unlock the door and shoot Thorne the moment the music stops."

"Unseen in the darkness, I silently return to my seat in the balcony. No one has even noticed I was gone."

The strains of Haydn played on, but the jollity of the music was at odds with the atmosphere of hostility in the Hall.

I walked over and shut off the tape.

Finally, one voice spoke up. Hard to see in the darkness, but I think it was Lisa DaPonto's.

"You said Thorne threw the only clue he could at you—a cuff link with a sharp sign—when he finally realized his danger. You even said that it might represent a set of initials. Are you telling us, Mr. Field, that he meant Hedda Hasse?"

I glanced over to the strained white face of the young singer.

"Exactly," I said softly. "That's exactly whom he meant."

26

You could feel the shock waves rise.

Murmurs of disbelief, at first. Then acceptance. Then relief.

"It had to be her! We should have known—"

"—the way she came in out of the blue like that—"

"I saw her walking off with the general near the canal last night—but I never thought—"

"—knew it couldn't be one of us—"

Lorenzo DaPonto rose at last, presumably to put the manacles on Hedda Hasse.

"Wait, Commissioner," I said. "There are still some gaps to be filled. She did indeed leave the Hall during the period of utter darkness—"

"I lost an earring! I slipped off to the open archway to find it. Surely the guard saw me—"

"There was no guard there," I said. "It's the one place in the entire auditorium where there was no guard. You must have gone around backstage and admitted the Marielito."

"There wasn't time! Even you can see that!"

I didn't like that "even you." But I ignored it and called on Rachael.

"Mrs. Radler, you were in Thorne's box last night with Ms. Hasse. Would you repeat what you heard Thorne say to her—the last words he said to anybody in this life?"

Rachael Radler stirred her considerable bulk and rose to her feet.

"He said 'Aren't you German?'—no, that's not quite right. What I think he said was, 'Aren't you European?' I believe he was surprised to see that a singer as good as Hedda was an American."

"No, that wouldn't have surprised him at all. America turns out the best-trained singers in the world. Didn't you say, though, that something interrupted Thorne?"

"He didn't finish the sentence. At least, I didn't hear it."

"Could he possibly have said, 'Aren't you a Yera'?"

Rachael looked astounded. She considered the possibility a moment, rolled it around in her mind, and replied, "You know, I think that is what he said. It just made no sense to me, so my mind supplied the missing syllables."

"Suppose he meant what he said?" I asked. "Thorne was the greatest living authority on Antonio Saul Yera. He must have collected every available photograph of him from infancy onward. He knew what he looked like as a younger man, though I didn't. Not until a friend referred me to a newspaper clipping dating back more than twenty years. He suggested I take a pen and sketch in more hair. I did. See who the picture looks like now."

I held up an enlarged photo of the real and younger Antonio Saul Yera. It was a full-face photo—with the composer holding up his hand to shield the face of the woman in the background. With a full halo of long, dark hair penned in, Yera's face was the spitting image of Hedda Hasse's. Even to the incandescent blue eyes that always come off, in a photo, as dead fish eyes.

"Yera—the real Yera—was forty-five years old when this picture was taken, with a full head of hair—dark hair, like Hedda's, though a common enough trait. More significant are those ice-blue eyes. Truly distinctive.

"But who in Fun City noticed the color of Yera's eyes? He was the New York composer who dropped down to Key Cohen now and then to check on Harmonia's construction. His wealth alone isolated him, then his 'grief.' Mayor had to begin his impersonation with a full wig, and he gradually reverted to his natural and advancing state of baldness. A fine disguise, since it can so alter a man's appearance. That and a great weight loss, explained away as a lingering illness, erased all memory of the true Yera's younger appearance. Ten years later, the impersonator could resume his conducting career, with no one the wiser.''

"Are you telling us," barked DaPonto, "that Hedda Hasse and this singer fellow—Mayor—did Thorne's murder together?''

"They had good reason to. Yera—Mayor, that is—was obviously smitten with Ms. Hasse. She spots him as an impostor. She has reason to believe she was the real Yera's illegitimate daughter—though until her parents' death she has no idea she was adopted. But what claim would a bastard child have to the Yera fortunes? Why not get it another way—through marriage? The money was theirs unless Mayor's real identity was uncovered. And the only one who could do that was Thorne. So Thorne was imported down here for the sole reason of killing him.''

"I didn't do it!" screamed a distraught Hedda. "You know I didn't do it!''

DaPonto seemed to think she did. To the surprise of no one, he read her her rights and led her out of the Hall of Mirrors.

Where the FBI took over.

27

THE party was over. No more movies. No more surprises. For the moment, no more explanations.

We straggled out of the Hall of Mirrors toward the open courtyard. The rains were so intense they had even wiped away all evidence of the splintered fountain sculpture. For that matter, there wasn't much left of the fountain, either, since the force of the bolt had landed squarely in this open space, merely glancing the South Tower on its way.

With no relief from the storm, it looked like another night in Harmonia, sans host this time. Somebody suggested a drink, everybody concurred, and we walked—a huddled mass—across the courtyard to Yera's wing. I mean, Mayor's. The uninvited settled into assorted chairs and watched a white-coated servant build a blazing fire. For such a normally boisterous group, the patrons were unusually subdued.

But then, so was I.

I stepped over to the long window and looked out on the storm. From here, I could see Hedda's white Mercedes convertible, as lonely and abandoned as its owner. No house-hunting with Hedda in that splendid chariot.

With drinks handed all round, the rest of the party was perking up. Myself, I was terribly depressed. Justice is one thing. Love—or simply infatuation?—quite another. But why

170

not call it by its proper name? It was love, all right. Love for all the Heddas in my life.

Rachael Radler joined me at the window and gave me a vigorous pinch on the buns. I leapt a mile.

"Cheer up," she said. "There are plenty more fish in the sea."

Oh good, I thought, nothing fixes you up like life's little adages.

"Too true, Rachael. It's always darkest before the dawn." And for good measure, I added, "Every cloud has a silver lining." When I am in total despair, I've noticed, clichés take over. Sometimes even before.

"Besides," continued my comforter, "yours isn't the only break-up here tonight. Look how Miguel and Connie are avoiding each other."

"Trouble in Paradise?" I asked.

"She'll be after you next. Come to think about it, she'll be after anybody next. I'd better get back to Dick. Don't stay over here. You're the star attraction tonight. And you still have a lot of explaining to do. So does Connie."

She took me by the hand and dragged me bodily to the center of the room.

"Sit on the floor. I'll bring some pillows. It's time we heard the whole story." Rachael cocked her head sideways and asked, "What is that awful racket?"

"Wind damage, I suppose," said the ever-practical Connie. "I'll have to check all my vacant listings first thing in the morning. Sit next to me, John—" She moved over two inches on her love seat, but I'd heard that song before and dived for the pillows on the floor.

"It's all beginning to fall together," said Commissioner DaPonto. "This Mayor fellow kidnapped his wife, took her out on a boat, and sunk the boat. His car was found with a suicide note inside—and everybody, police included, bought the story. That was before my time, of course, as police commissioner."

"It helped," I pointed out, "that Antonio Saul Yera identified the remains of his mistress and her former husband. Naturally, it wasn't Yera who did that—it was Mayor impersonating Yera. And what he identified were fragments of decomposed corpses that had washed ashore. Remember this supposed 'murder/suicide' occurred at the height of the first Cuban boatlift in 1961, and the waters from here to Cuba were filled with unidentified victims of drownings and shark attacks.

"On the plane, Thorne told me that Yera's grief and loss had forced him into seclusion in Florida. But Yera's impersonator would be very careful to carry off his deception far away from the people in New York City who knew Yera—and Jorge Carlos Mayor."

Lorenzo DaPonto preempted me at this point with his own summary of my deductions.

"So Jorge Carlos Mayor got vengeance and more besides. Not only did he kill his wife—"

"His ex-wife, you mean?"

He ignored me and went on. "He also killed her lover, Antonio Saul Yera, then began his impersonation, moved into Harmonia, and enjoyed the spoils. Quite a coup.

"Still," he added, "those murders will be hard to prove without a confession. So will Thorne's."

"No, Thorne's murder is quite easy to prove," I said. "There's the key to Thorne's box, for one thing. It was left on the doorsill. It's impounded evidence now, and it's being tested for fingerprints."

"Imagine a murderer forgetting an important piece of evidence like that!" Alicia Argento spoke up with her usual low-voiced enthusiasm.

"That's not too hard to imagine," I said. "I had the only set of keys to Harmonia—and even I forgot where I'd placed them initially. Then there's Harmonia itself. We don't have to say—'If these walls could only talk!' In this case, they have."

In the distance, we could hear a crash of granite and plaster above the sounds of the storm.

"What's happening out there?" The suave Robert O'Reilly looked genuinely alarmed.

"They've broken through" I said. "They've found the bodies."

"Who's broken through? What bodies?" Too late, the commissioner of police realized that not only was his turf stepped on it was being auctioned off for back taxes.

"The FBI," I answered, and I would have gladly amplified if DaPonto gave me the chance.

"What jurisdiction do they have in this case!" bellowed Fun City's police commissioner. "What right do they have to take over here?"

"I suggest you look at the bodies, Commissioner. They will tell you everything."

"You mean—" Lisa DaPonto spoke up at last. The white georgette of her gown matched the pallor of her face. "You mean the bodies are *here*? The bodies of Antonio Saul Yera and—"

"—and Hedda Hasse." I completed the sentence for her. "The music world knew her as Theresa von Trattner. The pianist who was once married to Jorge Carlos Mayor. Her real name—her maiden name—was Hedda Hasse. Hedda told me her grandmother had been married three times. During the course of the storm last night"—I colored slightly—"she even mentioned the names of her grandmother's husbands— Karl Hasse, Terrence Trattner, and somebody named 'Pick' Heinz. Heinz is not relevant to our story, but the other two husbands are. Two children were born of the first marriage— Hedda Theresa and Karl Aloysius. They were never formally adopted by Trattner, the second husband, but you can understand how a musician's management would latch with delight on a name like Theresa Trattner. All they had to do was add a *von,* and they had the name of a famous pianist who was a pupil of Mozart. Subliminal advertising. Legitimate, at that.

"Theresa used that name for her pianistic career, submitting to the wishes of her management. But when she composed—and she composed all her life—she used her real name. She even signed all her compositions with a sharp sign—two H's. A sort of shorthand. She adopted it as her personal symbol, her enigmatic signature. But then, she wove her entire name throughout her works, particularly in the so-called Yera Concerto.

"What you must understand is that the real Antonio Saul Yera never claimed those works as his own. That was the last—and the worst—act of revenge of a jealous and discarded husband. Yera did all he could to help her get her works performed. The premiere of her concerto—the Hasse Concerto, we'll have to call it now—was the last one he ever attended in Mexico City. I have no doubt but that he used all his influence to arrange for that performance. I also have no doubt that it was beyond the scope of the musicians to perform. We have to get these new sounds in our heads and fingers, you know—and nobody recognized its worth at the time. It was, fortunately, reviewed. James Goldman tracked that down for me.''

''You can straighten out music history later, Mr. Field,'' said Lorenzo DaPonto. ''Murder is what concerns us now, and I want to know why the hell the FBI has taken over my investigation!''

''Maybe they remember how you handled the first one,'' I suggested.

''You think they're going to prove anything from those bodies up there? I wish them luck! And all you've got as evidence for Thorne's murder is a key. Hell, a key can't even give you a full set of fingerprints!''

''No, but the sill above it can. That is the one thing the murderer forgot—to remove those fingerprints. Remember I mentioned, in our little play tonight, that I could manage to reach that doorsill, since it was a smaller replica. The real door is over seven feet high. Much too high for me. Too high for almost all of us.

''What you have to ask yourself''—I noticed a form moving toward the door, but I continued—''is one simple question.

''Where would a tall woman hide something?''

Constanze Weber—the tallest woman I knew—stood at the doorway.

''Don't attempt to follow me, any of you! You know me well enough. I'd shoot any one of you!''

Her voice had shed all pretense of a southern accent. It meant as much business as the dainty, pearl-handled Saturday Night Special in her hand.

28

I had no intention of following her.
Neither apparently had anyone else. They stood in stunned silence. Helpless.

Somebody wailed—Rachael, I think—"Where are those damned FBI agents when you really need them?"

I simply walked over to the window and watched.

Connie ran out into the driving rain and headed straight for Hedda's Mercedes. I knew the keys would be there. They always are.

I watched as she gunned the motor and raced off into the gloom.

"Somebody stop her, for God's sake!" Ochelly seemed to be looking at me.

From the window, I watched as the car veered out of control. Right near the canal where Sweeten had died. I watched as the car plunged into the water and sank slowly down and disappeared. And I remembered—last of all—her fear of tight, closed-in places. Like the narrow area above us where she had kidnapped, imprisoned, and shot her first two victims.

"It's too late," I said calmly. "There's no saving her now."

I left the room to look for Hedda.

29

"**Y**ou knew that car was sabotaged!"

Bill McIntire trapped me in the hallway. The rest of his FBI band went racing toward the canal. Bill himself was in a state of high—how shall I say?—dudgeon. Hair askelter. Eyes aflame. Angry.

"How could I know a thing like that?"

"Because you're not dumb! That's why!"

"I did think it odd, now that you mention it, that Connie and Tony—I mean Jorge—wanted me to go house-hunting with Hedda. That would have meant Connie would lose her commission. Totally unlike her."

"That's not all! Is it!" It's hard to take an FBI agent seriously when hair is blowing all over his face.

"Is that a question? Or a statement? Yes, I did suspect something else, I knew not what. But I am utterly blameless, since I passed that suspicion on to the local law enforcement officer, Lorenzo DaPonto."

"That charlatan!"

"I seem to recall a certain reluctance on your part to enter the case at all. It was only after my prowling around and proving a kidnapping—"

McIntire calmed down and brushed the hair out of his eyes.

"I apologize, John. I hate to have it end this way, that's all."

"It's the only way it could end. I'm glad it ended this way. Mayor would never have testified against her, you know. He was too afraid of her. Hit men penetrate prisons, too."

"I don't know," said McIntire. "After all these years, violent death still shakes me deeply. But you're not shedding any tears. You're not a merciful man, John."

"No," I conceded, "I am not a merciful man. Not where murder is concerned. But this, you know, was so much worse than murder."

McIntire and I stepped out to the driveway, and I bade him adieu.

The rains had stopped. As suddenly as they had begun.

It was going to be a fine night, after all.

30

ONE more night in Harmonia. Naturally, I can't sleep in my room. It's been all torn up with pickaxes, but I did go up to place several phone calls. No success at all there.

Well, I'm sure you've figured out the main plot, but let me just tidy up the details. I don't have long to do this. Paris tomorrow. Tonight—

As I mentioned, my own room is all torn up. I have this invitation to spend the night at the North Tower. You understand.

McIntire thought me cruel. And said so.

And it's true. I felt no mercy toward Constanze Weber. Not toward the woman who murdered a second Mozart. Not to someone who cut off that creative genius in her prime. At thirty-five. Just like Mozart. A lot like Mozart in other ways, too. Like Amadeus, we don't even know what Hedda Hasse looked like. All we have are vague descriptions, all of them different, all colored by varying perceptions. Not a picture survives. Nor a painting. Nor a snapshot. (I think back to that newspaper photo, with Yera holding his hand up to protect her, but even there, she had turned away. A woman without vanity, Mayor had recalled.) As I have said, I am not a fanciful man. But I don't think we're meant to know what she looked like. Her music speaks for her instead.

But I'm getting away from my story.

You think, I suppose, that I had a lot of apologies to offer Hedda? Hardly. That was all part of the act. I was waiting for one of the patrons to point out that my case against her had holes you could drive a truck through. (How, for example, could she steal a violin string at the same time as she was singing?) But that crew was so anxious to lay the blame on somebody—anybody—that they accepted the story gladly.

It was a ruse, of course, getting her out of there. As she well knew. The fact was, I didn't want her to learn the whole truth—about the bodies of her mother and father, I mean—just then. That task lies ahead of me tonight.

She knew nothing about her heritage, you see. Yera let that cat animal out of the bag when he said she was raised by an uncle. How did he know that? Unless, when she came to Florida (on a ninety-nine-dollar vacation, by the way, when they met by sheer chance), he put private detectives on her trail? He told me she was born in Frankfurt—which is not only a large city in Germany but an exceedingly small town in Kansas. How did he know where she was born, when she didn't? She thought she was born in Lawrence, Kansas, and she had no idea that her uncle and his wife were anything other than her real parents. As I suspected, Hedda was supposed to be on the plane that crashed with her parents. At the last minute, she couldn't make the flight.

I hate to admit it, but I was much too slow putting the pieces together on this case. Thorne was far quicker than I. (He had been right about the Hedda allusions in the music—wrong, of course, about *which* Hedda they referred to.) But Thorne was even noticing the homages to Hedda that abound in Harmonia—the window grilles, formal gardens, a poem set in mosaic tile. Mayor undoubtedly removed the statue of Hedda in the courtyard, never dreaming that far more damning evidence lay there.

My first clue was the music itself. In the heightened awareness of that charged performance, I saw the name ''Hedda Hasse'' highlighted in the original manuscript—actually set forth in red ink. And the original manuscript was doodled with sharp signs—all painstakingly filled in with Yera's initials by the time I saw it.* Then, in my night table, I found an old phone book—a very old phone book—with the same kind of doodling. This time, not filled in.

I can only attribute the second clue to a kindly Providence. A torn ticket stub was in the pocket of my borrowed tuxedo. The performer's name was destroyed, but the date and place— Mexico City, April 28, 1961—remained. So I had James Goldman check the records for a performance of Theresa von Trattner—or Hedda Hasse—for that day in Mexico City. He found a recital of H. Hasse works, led by a local conductor, in the conservatory archives on that date. It made sense that the real Antonio Yera would travel that distance with Hedda for that performance. It also made sense that the two might marry then, since her divorce had just come through.† Sure enough, the record of their marriage was registered the following day.

I think the two separated temporarily then—Yera back to New York to fill his musical commitments, Hedda to Kansas to have their child. In secrecy. It was vital that Jorge Mayor have no legal claim to that child, a claim he could easily make if the child were conceived while their marriage was still valid. And it was, after all, dissolved only a week before Antonio's and Hedda's marriage. She must have kept the truth even from her family. They assumed the child was Mayor's and that both mother and father died in the rigged murder-suicide. Hedda's brother and his wife shielded the child from the truth—or what they conceived as the truth (the real truth was even more horrible than they knew). They moved to new surroundings and raised young Hedda as their own.

Shortly after the birth, Hedda joined Yera at Harmonia, entrusting the baby to her brother. I believe they were trapped and killed there by Connie on or about July 26, 1961. That was the date of the newspaper photo that Connacht referred me to, and it was the last photograph before his long "retirement" in Florida. Mayor, by the way, was singing in London

---

* His "tick-tack-toe," as Yera called them.

† Eric Hanson confirmed this through a check of the public records in Albany. He also found Yera's decree nine months earlier. Both decrees were awarded on grounds of adultery, with Jorge Carlos Mayor and Constanze Weber, respectively, named as co-respondents.

then. He had no hand in the murders. He says he can prove
it, and I believe him.

He was willing enough to talk after Connie's demise. Connie called him and persuaded him to fake the murder-suicide.
Then to impersonate the composer and retire from the public
eye. Why not? His career had diminished to a few engagements, and he was dead broke.

The motive, of course, was money.

The whole point of the impersonation was for Connie and
Jorge to get their hands on the Yera millions. Not just Antonio's earned fortune but, more important, the immense sums
that Trujillo Yera had wrested, through blood and corruption,
from Salvanigua. Connie even met an ally—an innocent one—
in General Vance Sweeten, who would substantiate their claim
since he had known both father and son years before. By this
time, he could hardly see, though no one seemed to notice
that. Communications were reestablished between father and
son. Father comes over for a visit. Lo, he's assassinated on
the spot.

For over twenty years, things went smoothly. Then everything began to fall apart on them. First, Fun City decided to
build a bullet train right through Key Cohen. Connie and
Jorge warded off that threat by giving Harmonia away as an
arts center, with some strict provisions. Harmonia must never
be torn down nor altered in any way, even after the composer's death. No one must ever find out where the bodies are
buried.

Next, out of the blue, Hedda Hasse arrives on the scene.
They never even knew about her. The image of her dead
father and the legitimate heir to all the money they had con-
spired for. Did she know who she was? She didn't seem to.
Yet why was she here?

The important thing was to keep her here and then kill her
off. And my God, how they tried! One accident after another.
Yet none of them took. That broken foot, for example, was
a cable-car accident. But the cable didn't snap until the car
was five feet off the ground, and all Hedda got out of it was
a broken foot.

That child is indestructible! I will always believe that the
only reason we survived that flight down to Fun City was that
Hedda was on the plane. Connie thought she'd be killing off

two birds—Hedda and Thorne—with one stone. But never mind. She had a reserve plan all rehearsed, just in case of a hitch.

Why, you ask, was General Vance Sweeten killed? He couldn't even see whom he'd bumped into in the balcony hallway right after Thorne's murder. That's true. But there was Connie's perfume. Remember he said, "You're still wearing that godawful perfume, Connie!" She had just gotten it from Paris, and she bragged that she was the only one yet to have it. Sweeten's testimony could have hung her, so she acted quickly.

Miguel Ochelly, I should mention, was an undercover drug agent. He told me that Key Cohen is ideal for drug running, with all those coves and waterways, and that everybody but the Sweetens were engaged in it. Nothing big. Just nice pin money. Ochelly's affair with Connie was the price one must pay, now and then, in the line of duty. He realized—too late— that he'd been duped into aiding a murder by staying with Thorne in his box. He'd also been mildly sedated. Enough to doze off there, then to stagger back to his own box, where he fell asleep again. So he couldn't even testify to Connie's absence if he'd had to.

The irony of it all is that if Mayor hadn't been such a dedicated musician, Connie and he would have gotten away with the whole scheme. The money should have been enough for him. But it wasn't. He couldn't leave music alone. And to find score after score of Hedda's incomparable music left in Harmonia—well, it was just too much for him. He couldn't resist it.

Reminds me of something that Hedda (my Hedda) mentioned about Harmonia.

This is the house that Jack built, she said.

And then it goes on—

This is the malt that lay in the house that Jack built.

This is the rat that ate the malt that lay in the house that Jack built.

31

I was just straightening my tie.

It had been, and I say this in all modesty, a night to remember.

Hedda and I had been talking of this and that. And that and this. There were any number of digressions. She told me that she intended to give Harmonia to Fun City.

"Artswise," she said, "this city needs all the help it can get. And the memories are too painful for me."

"You're *giving* it away? You're not *selling* it? No more real estate? Ever?"

"It's not in my blood. It never was."

Well, we . . . um . . . chatted some more, and then I remembered that I did have that damn plane to catch.

"There's one more thing," I said, "that I have to clear up. It's really important."

I lingered over her mirrored reflection on the bed as I attacked the tie once more. I was having a lot of trouble with that tie.

"You said your grandparents kept trunks filled with music manuscripts. Compositions of their dead daughter, they told you."

"Yes. I used to rummage through them as a child."

"And you said your grandmother's third marriage was to a man named 'Pick' Heinz in Frankfurt, Kansas."

"That's right—fifty-seven varieties of pickles, you see."

"And that he's still alive—"

"He's eighty-seven--"

"—and living in Frankfurt. Well, I'm sure you appreciate the importance of those manuscripts."

"Of course. Musicologists will feast over them for years. Why? What's the problem?"

"The problem is this. Can you imagine how many Heinzes there are in a place called Frankfurt? I've called forty people already, and I still can't find—"

She laughed merrily and for some time.

"Oh, I see!" she said. "You think his name is spelled H-E-I-N-Z. Hasn't anyone ever told you there were as many Irish as German immigrants in Kansas? My grandfather's name is spelled H-Y-N-E-S.

"It's a play on words, you see. A pun." She was mirth itself. "You, of all people, missed that? You who love puns? You who figured out that Jorge Carlos Mayor was—"

Sometimes the only way to shut a woman up is simply to kiss her.

"All right," I said eventually. "The hoax's on me."

There was, fortunately, a later plane to Paris.